MY BEST FRIEND'S SISTER: SULTRY

BAD BOY ROCKERS #3

LEXI BUCHANAN

Published by HFCA Publishing House
http://www.lexibuchanan.com
http://ronajameson.com

SYNOPSIS

Growing up, if anyone had told Donavan that by the age of twenty-five, he'd be crazy about his best friend's little sister, he'd have laughed in their face. The reality is, he is crazy about her. She's beautiful with curves in all the right places, but that's not all there is to her. So, after two years of keeping his distance, he's not willing to do that anymore—he can't do that anymore.

Mara is eighteen years old, the middle of five girls, with an older brother who thinks he knows best. He's about to find out that he doesn't when she goes after his best friend. She's not blind and has seen the looks Donovan has thrown in her direction for the past few years, and she's sick and tired of waiting for him to make his move—a move he probably won't make without a push from her. Her only hope is that her brother doesn't do anything stupid to ruin his friendship with his best friend.

1

PROLOGUE

Mara

WATCHING MY BROTHER LEAVE WITH HIS GIRL makes me want to pack my bags and follow him—anything other than staying here with *him*. I've been in love with *him* for as long as I can remember. Yeah, I had a schoolgirl crush on him, but my feelings have grown into something more—into love. My heart breaks every time he says something that I don't want to hear. Like he doesn't want me here, well, that is something I know already without him shouting it at me. I mean he's been the most un-hospitable person ever.

Turning up on his doorstep in tears, you'd think that he'd have hugged me, but not Donovan. He'd clenched his jaw, opened the door wider so I could enter and then asked "What have you done now, Mara?" because it was me. I'd needed a hug and I'd needed someone to listen to me, but he wasn't willing to do either.

Ever since I turned sixteen he's kept his distance and always stays well out of my way when he comes home with the guys and visits with Reece. It hurts. It hurts a lot.

Out of the three musketeers, Donovan is the most laid back, but not with me. With me, he acts like I have the plague or something.

Since the door shut behind my brother, Donovan's been standing across the room alternatively glaring at me and looking out of the window.

My bedroom is calling because all I want to do is lock myself away and cry. He's never going to look at me the way I want him to. I can't stay here anymore. I've only been here a few days, but I can't stay here and watch him be with someone else. It'll hurt too much. And he's made it clear that he doesn't want me and never will.

A tear escapes as I quickly get to my feet and make for my room.

"Mara?"

I stop with my hand on the door handle refusing to look back at him. "What?"

Goose bumps form on my arms as I feel him walk up behind me, a breath away from touching me. It's difficult to breathe with him being so close. I rest my forehead against the door as Donovan surrounds me with his heat, resting his forearms at either side of my head causing his chest to rest softly against my back.

"Mara, I'm going to move out." He clears his throat. "I've already found somewhere so I'll be leaving in about a week."

My breath catches in my throat because I wasn't expecting him to say that.

"It's not right, us both living here together without Reece being here. People will get the wrong idea. Mara, please look at me."

Shaking my head, a shiver runs through my body when he nuzzles into my hair and breathes on my neck. It feels as though he's about to kiss me or it might be wishful thinking on my part.

"I'm too old for you," he whispers so close to my ear that lightening shoots straight to my core and my nipples pucker, desperate for his touch. "Mara," he trails along my neck with his lips, "are you listening to me?" He nips my earlobe with his teeth as his hand lands on my hip.

"Mmm," I reply, breathless.

Releasing the handle, I place both my hands on

the door in front of me and push back slightly, making full body contact with Donovan, who sounds as though the air has just left his body. He's solid against me. Rock hard and I don't just mean his abs.

The hand on my hip slides around and he splays his fingers against my belly, which is fluttering with butterflies. His other hand covers mine on the door as our fingers entwine. I've never felt so hot, wet, aching and aroused.

Donovan drops his head to the curve of my neck and breathes—heavily. "You're killing me."

He briefly presses me closer to him before letting me go, albeit reluctantly.

"I'm sorry. I can't do this. It won't happen again," he apologizes and then I hear his bedroom door slam shut.

My tears start to flow from my eyes as I slowly push my way into my bedroom and closing the door behind me, I lie across the bed and cry.

Now I know he isn't indifferent to me, it's going to hurt all the more knowing he isn't willing to do anything about it.

Donovan

Fuck!

I slam into my bedroom and just stand in the middle of the room not knowing what the fuck to do with myself. I promised Reece I'd stay away from his sister and what do I go and do? I go and practically pin her to the door with every intention of loving her. *Loving her.*

She's Reece's baby sister and is a total no. I've managed to keep her at a distance for years, but the fact is, she drives me totally insane and only has to look in my direction to give me an erection from hell. She thinks or rather thought that I don't like her, but the truth is I'm fucking obsessed with her. I'm obsessed with an eighteen year old virgin. At least I presume she's a virgin. I scowl at the thought of anyone else touching her because she belongs with me. *Dammit to hell!*

Dropping down on top of my bed, I catch my breath because I'd forgotten about the problem in my jeans, which I refuse to take care of myself. If I took care of it I wouldn't get the relief that I'd get between her sexy thighs so why settle for second best.

My erection throbs so rolling over onto my back I hope for some kind of relief while I clear my thoughts of Mara. *Sweet Mara.*

Fuck this.

Jumping up from the bed and grabbing my gym bag, I walk back out into the living area and hunt around for my sneakers, which I kicked off when I'd crashed out on the sofa last night.

Spotting them under one of the stools at the breakfast bar, I drop my bag and I'm about to reach for them when I spot Mara standing just outside her bedroom door watching me.

Wondering what the hell is going through her mind as she continues to watch me, I reach down and collect my sneakers, tossing them into my bag.

She looks lost, which makes my heart drop like stone to my feet. All I want to do is walk over to where she's standing and wrap her up in my arms and tell her I'm never letting go, but instead, I turn my back on her pretending to look for my keys, which I know are in the dish by the door.

"Donovan, you can stop ignoring me. I know this is awkward, but it's only a week, right? We're both adults so I'm sure we can act like it." She turns away, but not before I watch her wipe a tear from her face. Making me feel like the biggest jerk around.

After promising Reece I'd stay away from his little sister three years ago, I'd gone and led with my heart. If she has any of the feelings that I have for her then she's feeling crushed as though a vice is crushing her heart because that's how I'm feeling.

"Mara?"

"Please Donovan. Let's just try and forget what happened earlier and move on. I start school on Monday so I'll make new friends my own age. You don't have anything to worry about." She disappears into her bedroom, closing the door behind her.

Make friends my own age. You don't have anything to worry about.

Her words have frozen me to the spot as I feel my anger slowly rising. I'll kill any fucker who so much as looks in her direction and look they will, with her long dark hair, slim curvy figure and legs that seem to go on for miles even though she's shorter than me. She's the most beautiful woman I've ever seen and the only woman that's ever taken root in my heart apart from my mother. She's also the only woman that I can't be with, and that tears me in two.

2

MARA

4 WEEKS LATER

Standing alone, I'm finding it difficult to enjoy myself despite the pride of seeing my own paintings on display. This particular one I'm standing in front of was a labor of love that took me two weeks to finish. It's a central piece in my first showing and the whole show is something to celebrate. So why are the butterflies dancing in my belly ruining the celebration for me? I've never been so nervous before, and having Harry as my date for the evening isn't helping. He's great to talk to as a friend, but that's all we are—friends. My heart is already spoken for and I'm not sure I'll ever get it back.

How cliché is it that I've fallen for one of my brother's best friends? Someone who, up until four weeks ago, I'd thought couldn't stand me. Someone I thought didn't want me around. Discovering that he is attracted to me, but refusing to do anything about it breaks my heart, but not as much as seeing him arrive here at the art show with a skinny blonde on his arm.

Harry is my date tonight, I remind myself again. I shouldn't really be upset that Donovan has a date, but I am. I want to be the one holding on to his arm. I want to be the one to have his arms around me—his hands touching me.

Donovan has hardly been around since he moved out of the apartment he shared with my brother, Reece. I'm still living there, and would you believe my bedroom is Donovan's old one. Reece and Callie are in their room, and because of this I've been sleeping a lot with cotton balls in my ears. It kind of makes me sick listening to my brother having sex, but I feel safer in the city when Reece is close by and I don't fancy my chances on my own. Mom keeps telling me she's sorry for blaming me over the Dahlia situation and that I can go back home. The thing is I don't want to go back. Even though it hurts to stay, this is where I need to be.

Donovan might not come around the apartment that often, but I see him in the bar, which isn't too far away. I'm still underage to drink, but the owner allows me inside because of the guys as long as no one serves me alcohol. It pisses me off though because Donovan always makes time to chat with the groupies that hang around him, but he doesn't seem to have the time to chat with me—it hurts—a lot.

Sometimes I spend a lot of time standing in front of my mirror wondering what they have that I don't. My skin is smooth with even features, and is slightly darker than my normal ivory tone because of my time spent in the sun. My skin tone though brings out the rich greens of my eyes. I've been told they are unique and that they have a bright glow about them. But despite everyone commenting on my eyes, my favorite feature is my lips, which are full and plump—kissable.

Growing up, as soon as I developed an interest in boys, or rather one in particular, I'd practice using my lips by puckering up and kissing my mirror. Myself and Jenny, my best friend, also used to practice on bananas after Jenny had overheard her older brother on the phone gloating to his friend that his girlfriend had given him the best blowjob he'd ever had. Of course we snuck onto the Internet to find out what a blowjob actually was, and the pictures that came up made us both want to hurl—more so when Jenny reminded me that her brother loved getting one. We were fourteen.

Even though we practiced on bananas back then, I've still yet to put my practice into experience. I'm not a nun, but I've never wanted to touch anyone's dick until Donovan. So I guess you can say I'm saving myself for him, although I'm beginning to suspect I'll probably die a nun.

I know I'm desired. Boys my age are always asking me out. They tell me they love my hair, which is thick, curly and floats in waves down my back. But the problem is that they always seemed too young for me. The last boy I tried to go out with came in his jeans after one, hot make out session. He'd been kissing me while grinding against my leg. As he started to slide his fingers through my hair, he'd come. It was damn embarrassing for the both of us. I still can't look him in the eye.

But Donovan, he likes my legs. Oh yes, I've caught him looking more times than I can count. My legs are long and slim, even toned now that I tend to walk to the college and sometimes run between classes thanks to my bad time management skills. I've never caught him looking at my boobs though. Most guys look at them and talk to them, which on the odd occasion have gotten them a heel on their toe or a knee to their junk.

"Hey, sis," Reece says, bringing me abruptly

back to the present with his words and an arm around my shoulders.

I inhale and try to pull myself together. I'm supposed to be having fun, not getting lost in the past.

Slipping my arm around my brother, I snuggle into him, just needing to be held by someone I know loves me.

"What's going on Mara? You've been looking forward to tonight for the past week." He kisses me on top of my head.

"I'm fine really," I tell him knowing my words aren't that reassuring. "Just lost in thought."

"Mara—"

"Hey," Donovan interrupts. "Great work, Mara."

Reece keeps his arm around me, but turns so we're facing Donovan and *her*. None of us speak— we just stare. My heart flutters in my chest before splitting in half when I watch Donovan smile down at the woman whose hand is wrapped tightly in his.

Clearing his throat, Reece gives me a quick squeeze before releasing me. His smile is reassuring as Callie walks over to him and he gathers her into his arms. I'm surprised my brother came over to me without her because these days they seem to be joined at the hip.

"I have something to say," Reece states.

Then the rock on Callie's finger comes into view and Reece gets let off the hook.

"Oh my God. You're engaged." I grab Callie's hand, bringing it up closer to my eyes. "You're really engaged?" I ask looking between the two of them.

"Oh yes."

I've never seen my brother as sappy as he is when he's with Callie. In fact, it's really funny to watch and on a few occasion it's made me want to hurl, but I'm really pleased for them. I love Callie and she's really good for my brother.

"Congratulations," I offer, pulling Callie out of my brother's arms and into mine. Tears sting my eyes—a strange mixture of happiness for my brother and sadness that I'll never experience the same happiness with Donovan. "Thank you for making my brother happy."

"He's made me happy as well," Callie responds. "I've never met anyone like him before, and very soon he really is going to be mine. I can't wait." She squeezes me before being pulled into Donovan's arms.

No sooner am I free than Reece is standing in front of me wearing a frown on his face. "Mara, you're worrying me."

Reaching up, I wrap my arms around his neck,

and kiss him on the cheek, before saying, "I love you, and I'm really happy you've gotten your act together. Callie's good for you."

"Yes, she is." Reece grins and gently releases me before taking his girl back into his arms.

Out of the corner of my eye, I notice Donovan's gaze wandering to me.

He's watching me, more openly than he normally does. *What's going on with him?* It doesn't last long though because his attention is now on *his* date. I've no idea who she is and I'm not too sure I want to know. If I have her name and more details then it will make him being with someone else more real and I don't think I can deal with that.

When he looks at me my skin always prickles as though my body recognizes him when he's close. I can be talking to someone else with my back to the door, and the minute he walks in, I immediately know he's there. Sometimes I wonder whether he has the same reaction to me. There is something between us even though Donovan doesn't want to act on that something.

Taking a glass of some sparkling fruit drink as the waiter passes, I glance at Donovan again and let a small smile play on my lips when I see the frown on the girls face. She isn't happy. Now her hands go to her hips as she whispers something frantically to Donovan. He looks pissed.

My heart would soar to the stars if Donovan were to become my guy. To have him only look at me the way he did at the beginning to that *girl*.

Harry looks at me that way, which has started to make me feel uncomfortable. He's a really nice guy and I do enjoy spending time with him, but he isn't Donovan. It isn't fair to keep spending time with Harry when I'm sure he's expecting more from me. Trying to talk to him and tell him I'm only interested in friendship though hasn't been working out too good. He always seems to avoid the conversation by finding a distraction—a report to write or an errand to run. This tells me he knows what I'm going to say, but I hope he knows how much I want him as a friend. Anything else just isn't possible.

"Mara, wake up." Harry nudges me out of my daydream, sloshing my drink over the top of the glass onto the girl with Donovan.

"You bitch," she cusses, her pretty face twisting into an ugly snarl as she tries to dab at the stain on her dress.

"Sue," Donovan quietly whispers. "Apologize to Mara right now."

I was about to apologize to her until she cussed at me. It was an accident that didn't warrant such name-calling. Sue's face is red with anger and her blue eyes sweep over me with disdain. I swear she looks ready to hit me. And Donovan looks ready to throttle her.

"I said apologize to her. That was uncalled for."

"Donovan." He meets my gaze and the rest of what I was about to say floats straight out of my head. Tears prickle at the back of my eyes as the full force of her resentment hits me like a slap to the face.

"What the fuck is going on?" Reece demands. And I know from his tone and the glare he's throwing at her that he heard every word she said. "You need to leave. No one speaks to my sister like that."

"So, it's okay for her to throw wine all over someone deliberately? Is that what you're telling me?"

Callie pushes past Reece and goes right into Sue's face. "It was an accident."

"Look everyone. Can we calm down? I'm sorry okay. This is my entire fault for nudging Mara. I'm sorry," Harry interrupts, shocking everyone into silence.

"C'mon. I'll take you home." Donovan grabs Sue's arm and starts to drag her out of the room.

My heart feels heavy watching him leave with

his hand on her. I know he's only trying to get her out of here, but it still hurts.

The night is ruined for me now, and with Reece's arms around me in comfort, I still want to leave. My bed is waiting for me to crawl into it, and only then will I let my tears fall.

3

DONOVAN

Bringing Sue to the art show at the museum has to be one of the most idiotic ideas that I've ever had. Knowing Mara was taking *Harry* had pushed me in to finding someone as a date when really I should have gone alone. But being around Mara isn't something I'm able to handle alone any more. Every day my will to stay away from her is slowly disappearing.

Mara is my best friend's sister. And to make it worse, she is eight years my junior. But she's the only girl ever to get under my skin—a place she's been for a couple of years now.

Reece would be on me in two seconds flat if I ever made a move on his baby sister. I've always been around Reece and his sisters, but it was Mara's sixteenth birthday when she'd literally knocked the breath out of me. That was the day everything between us started to become awkward. As a result, I gradually spent less and less time at Reece's house just to avoid Mara.

At the time I'd freaked because of the age difference between us. So not right. Even now I can't decide which bothers me the most, the age difference or that she's Reece's sister.

After dropping Sue off at her place, I'm now sitting in my truck outside Mara's apartment building—my old apartment. Sue hadn't been happy with me dumping her at home and leaving. She'd made it clear that I could have everything else but that wasn't on the cards. Boy, was she pissed when she discovered this little fact. My only thought was to get back to Mara to make sure she's okay. The look on her face when Sue called her a *bitch* is on a loop in my head, which is why I'm sitting here trying to decide whether or not to go inside. If I do, Reece isn't going to be too happy to see me there, checking on his sister, but at the same time I'm not going to settle until I've seen her for myself.

Climbing out from behind the wheel, I slowly head into the building using the key I still have.

The scent of fresh paint burns my nose and I

grunt in displeasure. I hate the smell but I have to admit that the pale yellow walls and white trim is exactly what the building needed. The building only has four stories with Reece, Callie and Mara being on the third. Pushing my way through the door that leads to the stairwell, I notice these walls have been repainted white, making it seem so much lighter than the previous color of brown did. I always used to hate walking up these stairs—damn depressing.

Walking out on the third floor to another freshly painted hallway, I lift my head and freeze. Mara has her back against the wall to the side of the door with Harry standing in front of her—not an inch between the two of them.

That is so not fuckin' happening!

"What's going on?" I demand, my voice tight with anger.

Mara and Harry both turn their heads and watch as I walk closer to them. Harry swallows a few times and starts that nervous twitch he has going on with his fingers. Ignoring him, I meet Mara's stare and watch as for a split second her eyes light up with hope before the light goes out.

I'm not stupid and know she's attracted to me—this isn't me being vain either. A few weeks ago I'd had her in my arms after she'd had a run in with

Reece and I'd felt her quiver against me. I'd wanted nothing more than to pick her up and carry her into my bedroom, but I hadn't. When she was back home in Alabama I had peace, but now, I constantly have to sit back and watch her with other guys who wanted one thing from her. I have a feeling that Harry wants more than to get into her little panties, and that's killing me. If I continue pushing her away she's going to end up with someone like him. That should make me happy for her, except the thought of her being with someone else tears me in two. So I guess I'm not there yet, and I'm not sure I ever will be.

"You going to speak or stand there glaring at me all night?" Mara asks, stepping away from Harry.

Rubbing my forehead, I look between the two of them and smile inwardly when Harry starts to edge toward the stairwell.

"I'll call you tomorrow, Mara. Bye." Harry hesitates, his gaze sweeping toward me before he quickly runs back to her. After giving her a quick kiss, he heads toward the stairs, leaving me alone with her. With my girl. *Fuck!*

"Where's you're date?" Mara asks as she crosses her arms, which pushes her breasts up making her cleavage deeper.

I bite back a groan, and answer, "She's back at

her apartment." I take a step closer. "My only thought was to check on you. Are you okay?"

After a second or two of silence, she nods. "Yeah. I'm okay."

I hear what she's saying, but I really don't believe her because she won't meet my eyes.

"Mara," I step into her space, "don't lie to me. I've known you for years and I know when you're lying."

When she finally meets my gaze, I watch as a lone tears slips down her face and I long to wipe it away. She looks everywhere, her gaze going back to some unseen hurt. "I was looking forward to the show tonight, but you showed up with her, and then, well, I just wanted to be home."

Showing up tonight with Sue had been self preservation if I'm totally honest, and knowing I hurt Mara and made her sad when she should have been having a good time is like a kick to the gut. Unable to keep my hands to myself any longer, I reach out and taking hold of her arms, I pull her into mine.

She buries her face into my chest as I wrap my arms tightly around her, holding her against me. Seeing her upset hurts—it hurts a lot.

"Mara, babe." I slide my fingers through her

dark curls and hold her face against me as I bend my head and rest my mouth against the top of her head. Mara's hair smells of fresh flowers and I breathe it in deeply as I kiss the top of her head. "I'm sorry. I only brought her with me to stop me from getting closer to you but here we are."

Mara lifts her tear stained face—her eyes questioning. I cup her face in my hands and use my thumbs to brush them away. Without thinking, I bend and kiss her cheek to catch a wayward tear. She inhales as I freeze. *I shouldn't have done that!*

Our lips are mere inches apart. My heart feels like it's about to explode through my chest. I want nothing more than to close the gap between us, to finally taste her. Instead, I push her away from me and clear my throat.

I brush the loose hair behind her ear before pulling my hand back and shoving it in to my pocket. "Go inside Mara, and I'll see you later." I need to learn to keep my hands to myself.

"Why?" she asks.

"You know why. *Dammit!*" I shove my hands through my hair, frustration ripping through me. I want to be with her but we both know why I can't. Just as I turn away, the apartment door opens and Callie appears from behind it.

She looks over her shoulder before looking between the two of us. "You coming in?" Callie opens the door wider so Mara can enter, but I take a step back.

"I'll see you both later," I whisper, hoping Reece doesn't hear me. I can do without him throwing his suspicions out at me right now. Especially when the suspicions would be spot on.

Callie doesn't say anything as I make a dash for the stairwell to head home to my empty, dark apartment. I suppose it isn't as bad as I make it out to be. It's a large open space for the living part with a separate room for a bedroom, office and bathroom. It's just too damn quiet being on my own after spending a few years rooming with Reece.

Recently, I've been thinking about moving back home. I own a large, empty house that is peaceful and secluded. I can lie out on the deck and just listen to the sounds of living in the country—the gentle breeze that rustles the leaves on the trees and bushes. Even the early morning wake up calls from the birds would be peaceful. It would certainly be better than waking up here to truck horns, as the drivers get impatient in early morning traffic.

I really don't know what the fuck to do any more. When my parents were killed in the car crash and I suddenly found myself alone, it was Jack,

Reece and their families that helped me keep my shit together. So pursuing this thing that's between Mara and me isn't something that we could go into lightly. We're practically family and I already know Reece's feelings on the subject, and Mara's mother wouldn't be too happy either or would she?

4

MARA

'We're going home."

"What? No way. You go with Callie. I'm staying here."

"Mara, stop being damn stubborn. Mom's apologized for blaming you, and I thought you were cool with that," Reece says, frustration clear in his voice.

"I am okay with that, but I'm happy here and I don't want to go home. Besides, I'm in the middle of my art course. I can't just get up and leave on a whim."

Reece is driving me crazy. For the past couple of weeks, since the art show, he's been acting all weird. Today, he's been hovering around as though he wants to say something to me, but doesn't have the courage—and now I know why. Things at home will probably be strained if I go back. I'd much rather give Mom a wide berth for now after the things she accused me of. It really hurt when she said it was my fault Dad had gone and fucked someone else. Then he'd gone and gotten that someone pregnant and the result was Dahlia being born. It was messed up because I wasn't even born then. All these years no one had known, except for Reece, but I'd been the one who had gotten the blame because I had been the only one home when Mom had discovered *Dahlia*. So although Mom may apologize every time we speak, which isn't often, I'm still not ready to go back and face her.

My eldest sister, Amanda, has been on me about coming home. She was positive that the first homecoming would resolve the problems and I would finally have it off my mind. The thing is, it isn't playing on my mind all the time. My head is so full of my art course that I don't have time to think about other things. When I do give my brain a rest, in slides Donovan. My family, although I love them, aren't really on my mind 24/7, but I've no wish to say that out loud to Amanda. She's very much like our mother with what comes out of her mouth and her mannerisms.

Now that she's finished college, she's moved back home while she works in the new law firm in town. If you ask me she's only doing all this because she has her eye on marrying someone who can give her the life she wants, and that she's set her sights on the new lawyer. He is kind of cute in an older man kinda way.

"For *God's sake* Mara! Stop switching off and listen to what I'm saying." Reece snarls, his lips twisted in anger.

He is definitely pissed that I keep tuning him out.

"Will you answer me?" he growls.

I guess I should be listening to what he's saying instead of daydreaming.

"I didn't catch what you asked me."

"Fuck." He stomps off toward the window while running his hands through his dark hair.

I snicker.

"This isn't funny." He turns to face me. "Are you listening this time?"

Nodding, I bite my lip to stop the grin from spreading across my face.

"I was saying that your art course is only a week in to the six week program. That means you can start the other one, which is starting up in two weeks when we get back. So my question was, will you be okay with traveling back with Donovan be-cause I'm taking Callie on my bike? And before you say anything, going home isn't really negotiable because Jack and Thalia have decided to move their wedding forward and it's happening next weekend."

News about the wedding makes me stop and think. I love weddings, which reminds me to check my phone. I'd received a message from Thalia titled 'Wedding,' but I'd been running late for class and with everything else happening, I'd forgotten to read it.

"What are you doing now?"

"Thalia, texted me before but I forgot to read it."

Grabbing my phone, I unlock the screen and bring up Thalia's message. The scream I issue makes Reece jump and I almost laugh.

Running over to my brother, I throw myself into his arms and say, "I'm going to be a bridesmaid." Jumping out of his arms just as quickly as I jumped into them, I dash toward my bedroom. "I'm going to pack."

"Fuckin' hell Mara, is that all I had to tell you to get you to agree? I really don't understand women," he mumbles, following me into my bedroom.

"Look, we both know why I'm not too keen on heading home, but if there is a wedding happening then hopefully there will be more to do than sitting at home with Mom."

As I grab my bag from the top of the closet, it suddenly dawns on me that I'm probably not the only one going home for the wedding.

"Is everyone coming home?"

"Yeah. Why?"

This should be fun. "No reason."

That means my sister, Sarah, will be home as well. She's had a crush on Donovan about as long as I have and she's two years older than me—that's two years closer to Donovan's age.

I'm not going to worry about her right now because we do have a sister code, and she won't go after the same guy I'm in love with. *But she doesn't know you're in love with Donovan.*

Sighing and shoving the thought of my sister and Donovan out of my head for now, I open the drawers on my dresser before turning back to Reece. "Can you go and do something else while I pack? I'd rather not have my brother seeing my bras and panties."

I grin as a look of pure horror fills Reece's face and he races from my room before slamming my door behind him.

My clothes tend to be more toward comfort than fashion. I practically live in jeans, and back home, I live in those as well as shorts. But my underwear, I have a tendency to splurge. All my panties and bras were bought from Victoria Secrets with my hard-earned cash.

For the past two years, I've been blogging. At first it started out as a way to pass time, but my reviews of art books and art shows I've attended has really taken off. *Mara's Thoughts* has over sixty-seven thousand followers, which makes my heart flutter every time I think about it. I'm not sure how that happened, but I'm not about to ignore something that I'm good at—something that I'm respected for. I'm not sure how people would feel if they ever discovered I'm only eighteen and that I was sixteen when I started the blog. My family are still unaware of my hobby or job.

About seven months ago, a publisher approached me and asked for rates for art book reviews as well as reviews for fiction novels set around the art world. Of course being seventeen, and constantly having to ask my mom for money every time I needed something or every time I was going out with friends, I jumped at the opportunity to get paid for doing what I love. And it's a publisher who is paying me so it's not like I'm taking money from the actual author, right? I'm also honest with my reviews even when it's a paid review. If I don't like the book, I say so.

The fiction novels certainly opened my eyes to the world of sex and eroticism. My mind had boggled reading some of the scenes in the books they'd sent me. I'm so glad that they had no idea of my age otherwise I'd have missed out on some very steamy lessons in what a guy likes, and what he can do with his tongue and dick. I have one word to describe them—*fuckin' hot*—okay, maybe two words.

Donovan is going to have a shock when he discovers what I know. I've never wanted to practice on anyone but Donovan. To be honest, I can be shy by nature, but something tells me I'm going to be too lost in the man to worry about being shy. And now I get to spend hours in the car with him while he drives me home. I'm not even going to ask him if he wants me to share the driving because I know what his answer will be. One very big, fat NO! He's rather possessive about his truck. And yes, I'm rolling my eyes.

5

DONOVAN

TURNING DOWN THE ROAD TO MARA'S apartment to pick her up, I spot a space directly out front, which doesn't happen often. Much to the annoyance of the car that comes up behind me, I reverse into the space and spot the woman of my obsession struggling through the front door with her suitcase and bag.

Jumping out of my truck, I run over and help her by taking the suitcase out of her hands.

"I've got this," I say, pulling it the rest of the way through the door.

"Thanks. The door keeps sticking."

"It always has."

She turns her face up to look at me, but not before I catch the scent of her perfume.

Very subtle, but it's there teasing my nostrils. I'm going to be damned uncomfortable on our ride back south, and I'm not talking a couple of hours here. It's probably going to take us about seven hours to reach our destination, which is why I wanted to get going so early in the morning.

Now I have my fresh-faced beauty standing in front of me with a smile on her lips as she waits for me to get moving. But I can't move, instead, I'm blocking her way with my feet feeling like lead.

"I thought you wanted an early start," she comments, tilting her head to one side as she observes me.

"Um, yeah." I turn away and put one foot in front of the other back to my truck.

Her soft footfalls behind me tell me she's following. My only hope is that I can pull myself together before we're cooped up in the truck all day. It's going to be a long drive trying to keep my distance from her. I'm not sure why Reece suddenly decided it was cool for me to hang with his 'out of bounds' sister, but apparently it is.

If I can manage to bury the lust to have this woman as my own then I'm planning on enjoying my time with her because I might not get the chance again.

She's beautiful today, as always, and looks stunning and fresh. Her dark curls have been left down, and if I close my eyes, I see my fingers sliding through her lengths as I wrap the strands around my hands while I slowly make love to her.

I try to shake the image from my mind. These are the kind of thoughts that I need to keep for when I have privacy and not when I'm opening the back door of my truck to toss her stuff inside.

"Do you want me to put your bag in here as well?" I ask, keeping my back to her so she doesn't see the bulge in the front of my jeans.

"That would good. I don't need anything out of it."

She hands me her bag, which I store in the back before shutting the door. As I turn to get into the truck, she's still standing behind me.

"Are you okay?" she asks.

"Yeah." I laugh to hide my embarrassment. "Why wouldn't I be?"

"Um," she glances down, "no reason."

With a smirk on her face, she walks around to the passenger side and climbs in while I'm left cussing—me and my fuckin' dick.

Slamming into the truck, I pull out into light traffic while I try to get my thoughts off a naked Mara and onto our destination.

Mara's sisters will be there, hounding me as

usual, but this time I'm more nervous about being around them than before. Sarah, Mara's slightly older sister has been texting me on and off lately. I've kept it to one-word answers—not wanting to get drawn into a conversation. She's like all Reece's sisters and when they set their sights on something or someone, everyone else better watch out.

The problem is the only girl I want to be with is Mara, and having one of her sisters trying to get more out of me isn't going to go down too well with anyone. I sure as hell don't want to cause conflict between the two sisters. They've had enough recently with the discovery of Dahlia to want or deserve any more. Reece wouldn't be too bothered, I don't think, if it was Sarah that I had it bad for, but he's close to Mara and always treats her as though she needs protection from me.

He has every right to be worried because he knows me and my appetites. I mean, you can't exactly share a woman and not know what a man whore your friend is, or should I say was.

Up until Reece got his shorts in a wad over Callie and asked me to take a step back, I've been having a dry spell. Although I suspect Mara turning up on my doorstep five weeks ago might have something to do with that.

She always pops into my head, but to have her

in front of me looking sexy-as-fuck killed my libido for anyone else. I'm so screwed.

Flexing my hands on the steering wheel, I briefly turn to glance at her. She looks comfortable surrounded by the plush leather seat. She is curled up with her shoes removed—if we were a couple, I'd be holding her hand right now.

My fingers twitch wanting to touch her. This is the first time we've been alone together for as long as I can remember, and, for the first time in history, I've no idea what to say. Before she moved here, when we were together we could talk and talk, but now it feels awkward between us. And I hate it.

I sigh. This is going to be a long drive but it's the perfect opportunity to bring our relationship back to what it should be—simply friends. It won't be easy but we need to try because I'm sick of walking on eggshells around her, especially when Reece is present.

With that in mind, I ask her, "So Harry was fine with you up and leaving as quickly as you have?"

Before she answers, I feel her eyes on me and fight the urge to look at her.

"I texted him last night after I realized Reece wanted me to go home with everyone because of the wedding. He wasn't happy when I told him I was travelling home with you." She shrugs her shoulders. "We're not dating so it shouldn't be a problem."

I'd already worked out that she wasn't dating him, but I feel relief hearing her confirm it.

With a quick glance at her, I catch the crinkle across her brow as she uses her fingers to rub her temples as though she has a headache.

"What's with the frown? Are you okay?"

She sighs. "Yeah, I'm fine."

"Hmm."

"What does 'hmm' mean?"

"I'm thinking you're not liking Harry as much as he likes you." I shouldn't say anything because I'm just going to piss her off all the more. At least we'll be talking—arguing, which is better than silence.

"Leave Harry out of this. He's a nice guy."

I snigger realizing she was probably about to say boy before she thought better of it.

"He's nice. At least he likes me."

She folds her arms across her chest, which I always try my hardest not to look at, but my eyes somehow find their way back. Mara isn't exactly small and when she crosses her arms, it kind of shoves 'em up. I've seen guys' eyes widen when they've been confronted with her.

Gripping the steering wheel, I say, "What's with the comment? I like you."

"Yeah. Right." Now I get the shoulder toss as she stares out of her window. "If you liked me, you wouldn't be avoiding me."

I swallow feeling like the biggest dick around. I want her. I want her so damn much that I've tried to stay away from her before I take what I want. I'm not just talking about taking her for a night. I'm talking every night. I want so much more than I've ever wanted before, and I want it all from her.

"I do like you, Mara." I sigh. "I like you too much, which is why I avoid you." I'm an idiot for telling her this, but the thought of her thinking I don't like her is unbearable. "Don't say anything, okay. I just wanted you to know that I don't hate you."

"I like you, too," she whispers after a minute.

I groan inwardly at what her words do to me. Instead of replying, I distract myself with traffic. This is one time I wish I'd kept my mouth shut, but losing my parents kinda made me realize that you won't always have tomorrow to say or do what you can't be bothered with today.

When my parents died, I was lost. In fact, I don't know what I would have done without her family.

Her mom basically held me together and made sure I ate. Reece and Jack were around me all the time like brothers and stopped me from drowning in despair. Losing someone you love is never easy whether you know it's about to happen or it's a total shock.

I'd be lying if I told anyone that I'm over it because I'm not. Driving back home, knowing my mom isn't going to be at home waiting with her apron on after baking up a storm that morning, is a pain straight to the heart. Knowing that my dad isn't going to be bugging the shit outta me about taking the boat out with him to fish is just as painful. Sure, the conversations were boring as shit, but I'd do that everyday for the rest of my life if it meant I had him back. Had both of them back.

6

MARA

SENSING DONOVAN'S MOOD SHIFT, I START TO look for somewhere to make a pit stop. Not only could I do with a bathroom break, but I'm also in need of another caffeine fix. The quick cup I had this morning was really too quick, not enough. At least it's an excuse to get him to pull off the road for a bit.

I'm not sure what's going on with him though. He seemed fine when we left, but since he admitted to liking me too much, he's been quiet. Not the travel in silence because we're at ease with each other, but the 'I'm about to lose it' silence. Pondering the tension between us, I almost yell in delight when I spot a coffee house. Not Starbucks, but right now coffee is coffee and I need to get Donovan to loosen back up. So with that in mind, I point out the window and say, "Let's pull over and grab some coffee."

He glances at me from the corner of his eye as he starts to indicate he's pulling over.

Why am I nervous now? I shouldn't be nervous with him but I am. It's always there, the attraction, just under the surface. I'm nervous with him off and on whenever he's around. Brooding, which he's doing right now, makes it worse. It definitely isn't helping to calm me down any.

Pulling into a parking slot, Donovan turns the ignition off and just sits staring out of the window. With a sigh, I open the door. Jumping out, I take a second to enjoy stretching my legs—it feels so good. Closing my eyes, I lift my face to the sun, and let the rays soak into my skin for a few minutes before I feel eyes on me.

Looking around, not too far away, I spot a guy who looks to fill his jeans and shirt pretty well staring at me. When he catches my gaze, he winks and starts walking toward me, but pauses mid-step. Catching movement beside me, I turn and see Donovan resting with his back against the truck staring the guy down.

I feel like kicking him.

I'll show him.

Turning back to the guy, I give him my megawatt smile, which gets him moving toward me again. He stops in front of me, and asks, "Is he your brother?"

"No." Then I add, "He's a friend of my brother whose been lumped with driving me home for a friend's wedding."

"Where's home?" he asks shuffling closer.

"None of your business," Donovan interrupts, glaring at the guy before he turns back to me, and says, "I thought you wanted a coffee."

"I do," I reply trying my best to hold eye contact with the new guy while I wonder if this is making Donovan jealous. "But I'm making a new friend."

"What—" Donovan ends on a cuss. "Well, why don't you let your new friend buy you a coffee while I go and take a leak?" And with that he stomps off around the side of the building.

Where the hell is he going? The restrooms are inside.

"Um. It was nice to kinda meet you, but I better go."

I don't give the guy a chance to respond because I take off after Donovan. I'd forgotten that the reason I'd wanted to stop was to try and get him out of the slump he'd suddenly fallen into, but I'd gotten sidetracked and hoped Donovan would act jealous.

Turning the corner to the diner, I spot him with his hands resting against the wall and his body pushed out with his head dropped between his shoulders. I slow my pace, but coming to a stop beside him, I reach out and place my palm on his back.

"Donovan, please tell me what's wrong."

He turns his head to the side his black hair falling over his eyes, which casts shadows over his chiseled cheekbones and plush lips as he meets my gaze, his blue eyes glowing in anger. "Where's your friend?"

I shake my head. "He isn't my friend, but you are," I answer, concern filling my heart.

My hand starts to caress up and down his back. Touching him, although innocently, feels so good, and by the shudder that I feel go through him, he feels the same way.

Donovan inhales and steps away from my touch, shoving his hands into his back pockets. "So, you want to go get that coffee?"

The stubborn ass.

"Not until you tell me what's going on. One minute you were fine, and the next you kind of tuned out and looked blank. As though you were having dark thoughts."

He seems to sag in front of me. "I'm sorry Mara. It's difficult, every time I head home, you know. But give me a couple of days at being back there and I'll be good again."

His parents. I'm an idiot. Donovan always seems so put together, more so than my brother or Jack, that I'd temporarily forgotten what he's lost.

Without thought to the consequences of getting too close to him, I take the steps separating us and wrap my arms around his waist. I rest my face against his chest and just hold him. A few seconds pass before he seems to wrestle with his shock and wraps his arms around me, pressing me closer to him.

"I'm sorry. I should have realized," I mumble into his chest.

He dips his head and kisses me on the top of my head before he says, "You don't have anything to be sorry for. It's just hard. Every time I pull up to the house, I expect to see my mom come running outside. I'm not sure that will ever change."

"I'm here for you. I'm always here for you, Donovan." I kiss his chest and feel movement lower. I'm arousing him. Well good, because he arouses me all the damn time. "Would it help if I came to your place first? We can have a drink and get the place aired some. Maybe it won't be as hard on you if I'm there with you."

"You'd do that for me?" He runs his fingers through my hair.

I tilt my head up to look at him. "I'd do pretty much anything for you," I whisper the truth.

Groaning, he drops his forehead to mine, and breathing heavily, he kisses my forehead. His hands momentarily tightening in my hair before he completely steps away.

"C'mon. Let's grab the coffee to go." He wraps his arm around my shoulders to get me moving before releasing me. "And thanks, but I'll be fine going home. I have to be."

Opening the door for me, I walk inside and let him lead me to the counter.

He doesn't have to be alone.

I'm guessing it's me that he doesn't want coming to his home—too much temptation.

Smiling, I take a sip of the coffee he's just passed to me. I have two weeks of living closely to him so who knows what can happen. Both my brother and Jack are going to be wrapped up in their girls for them to spend as much time as usual with Donovan. Oh, they'll still hang out together, just not as though they're joined at the hip like they usually do.

Reece won't like me hovering around Donovan, but my sister, Sarah, better get the message that he's mine.

I've seen the looks she gives him when she thinks no one else is watching, but I'm on to her. She may be my sister but I'm going to make sure she knows to stay clear. She's two years older than me, and that much closer to Donovan in age, but by the end of the two weeks, I'm determined to make him want me, and only me. I can be very persuasive when I have my heart set on something or someone.

7

DONOVAN

AFTER A SEVEN HOUR AND THIRTY-THREE minute journey, I'm home. Mara had tried to talk me in to letting her come home with me first, but I'd refused. She hasn't been with me in the past and she won't be with me in the future. This is something I have to do alone. The fact is I don't want the girl who has me tied in knots to witness my emotions as I walk into my home. I was raised here by two wonderful parents and I couldn't bring myself to come home with anyone. I have to do this alone. Tossing my bag into my room, I walk around checking the place out—everything looks as I left it. Coming back downstairs, I find Jack on the back porch with a beer in his hand—the remaining five on the table.

"Thought I'd come and welcome you back," he says, resting back with his feet on the table. "Actually I'm surprised you're back so soon."

I frown at his words.

"I thought you at least had the sense to stay over on the way back. I mean, it isn't often you get Mara alone for that length of time."

"What—"

"You have it bad for her." He gives me a shit-eating grin. "I don't think Reece realizes just how badly you want her."

Joining him with his feet on the table, I take a drink from the longneck I've opened, wondering what the heck I'm supposed to say to him. We're not a couple of girls ready to gossip, but I guess I need to say something. "Look. She's eighteen and Reece's sister, which makes her totally out of bounds."

Placing my feet back on the floor, I rest my elbows on my knees while watching the lake at the back of the house. "Sarah keeps texting me. Thought I might ask her out. She turns twenty-one soon so she won't be underage if I take her over to the bar for beer and fries."

Jack chokes on his beer. "Are you fuckin' with me? Because I'm telling you if you go anywhere near Sarah, you'll break Mara's heart."

My eyes snap back to him.

"I might only have eyes for Thalia, but it doesn't make me blind and that young babe has you on her mind. Don't screw with her feelings by asking Sarah out when you're not really interested in her. Reece really will be pissed if you do that."

Sighing, I say, "Reece will be pissed regardless of which sister I have my eyes on." I sit back and close my eyes with my head resting against the chair. "Mara would be more than a one night stand. I can't explain it, but she's under me."

He spits his beer out. "You wish," he says in choked laughter.

"What's up with him," Reece nods in Jack's direction while taking a beer. I jump and hope that Reece hadn't heard any of our conversation as he came around the house.

"Went down the wrong way." I'm sure as hell not telling him we were discussing his sisters—not ready for that conversation yet or ever!

"Thought you were taking your girl out," I comment, knocking more beer back.

"She's doing some girly shit with Thalia."

"Yeah, Thalia said something about going and getting waxed." Jack wiggles his eyebrows. "Love my girl naked, if you know what I mean." He grins. "I think Mara's tagged along as well."

I try not to react to Jack's comment, but I catch the glare Reece throws in my direction before looking back to Jack. "Can we leave my sister and waxing outta this conversation?" He shudders.

Mara hair free isn't something I want to think about while sitting out here with my two best friends. In the past, getting aroused in front of them would never bother me, but letting them see me hard while talking about Mara wouldn't go down too well with Reece—forever, the protective brother.

Changing the subject, I ask, "So, you ready to have a wife?"

"Wife," Jack moans resting his head back against the chair. "I've been ready from the day I met her." He looks me in the eyes. "When you meet the girl you're meant to spend the rest of your life with, you just want that wedding ring on her finger so every other fucker knows she's spoken for. Won't stop some, but the majority will take a step back. So yes, I'm ready to have a wife. To love, honor and cherish her till death do us part."

Listening to Jack speak from the heart has left me speechless. Jack is never vocal about his feelings for Thalia. Then again she's usually with him and no words are usually needed to describe how he feels about her because they're usually written all over his face.

"I think I'm gonna get Callie to marry me as well."

"Didn't you already ask her to marry you?"

"Donovan, don't be a dick. I meant I'm going to get her to marry me on the weekend when Jack and Thalia tie the knot," he grins.

I glance at Jack and see the same shock on his face that I'm sure is on mine. "You serious?"

"The more I think about it, the more I'm liking the idea that Jack put into my head. But you don't think Thalia would mind sharing her day with Callie and me."

"Are you friggin' kidding. They're best friends, plus Thalia may have mentioned it once or twice." He grins.

Both my friends getting married. *Wow*. I'm not too sure how this makes me feel. I'm obviously happy for them, but both married while I don't even have anyone special in my life. I have someone special in my life though—*Mara*.

Shaking myself out of the gloom I feel myself sinking into again, I grab another beer and find myself agreeing to be best man for Reece. Something I'm not sure they've thought about, and I can't believe I am, is a dress for Callie.

"I hate to burst your bubble, but what is Callie going to wear. She hasn't exactly had much time to get a dress and all the under-things they wear."

"You leave Callie's under-things out of your head."

"And don't even start on Thalia's under-things. Concentrate on," he pauses mid-speech. With a quick look from me to Reece, who tightens his hand on his bottle of beer, Jack carries on, "um, well, whoever." He cringes at his lame cover up. Unfortunately, I'm not sure it sailed passed Reece.

"I'm going to go and find Callie. We have a lot to talk about." He places his empty bottle on the table and nods at Jack before turning and standing in front of me. "You're one of my best friends. You're like a brother, which is why I'm going to say this nicely. Please stay away from Mara." And with that he's gone into the night.

"That went well," Jack comments.

"Yeah."

Sighing, I try to relax but I can't settle knowing how my best friend feels about me being with the girl I want with all my heart and soul.

If I hadn't been drinking, I'd go for a run, but the slightest bit of alcohol on my stomach usually knocks me sick when I'm running. I need something though, which is when I remember about the bag hanging in the basement. It's been a while since I've ventured downstairs, but right now I need to let off some steam before I explode.

Looking back to Jack, he's watching me with an expression I can't decipher.

"You've never been like this before," he observes. Placing his bottle on the table, he stands and walks over to me. "If it's meant to be then it'll work it's self out." He thumps me on the shoulder before jumping off the porch and heads to his car. "See you tomorrow. Tux fitting," he shouts over his shoulder and then he's gone.

I groan.

The thought of wearing a tux does nothing but causes my toes to curl. Don't get me wrong, I don't mind dressing up some but being confined in a tux all day isn't something I'd do for anyone other than a brother.

With a last glance across the lake to the houses lit up on the other side, I grab the empties and toss them into the trash. Grabbing the remaining bottle, I shove it in my fridge on the way through to the basement to work through my frustrations.

8

MARA

Biting my lip to keep my mouth shut is really starting to hurt. Not only is the woman who is pinning me into the dress I'm supposed to wear for the rehearsal dinner—when it's finalized—using me as a pin cushion, but my sister Sarah is whispering to our oldest sister, Amanda about a plan to get Donovan to notice her. *Over my dead body*! He's mine. He just needs to get over the age difference. I know he isn't immune to me. Now we're home, I'm going to make sure our paths cross more and more.

"Ouch."

"I'm sorry, Mara, but you need to stay still."

Ugh! I haven't even moved, and she's been pinning me for over thirty minutes now—first my bridesmaid dress and now this one.

Deciding for my own peace of mind to ignore Sarah, I glance into the mirror and find myself speechless. This morning I'd over slept after my evening out, and I'd just piled my hair up on the top of my head, but, looking back at myself now I look sexy.

The dark wine dress is made of silk, which falls over my curves perfectly. The silk is thin, which prevents me from wearing a bra and makes me feel uncomfortable. My breasts are more on the large side, although firm and perky so going without a bra isn't a problem, but it isn't something that I do. To make the dress look good though, I'm going to have to this time. At least my lacy thong isn't showing so I don't have to go completely naked beneath the cool fabric.

"Okay, Mara. You'll do. Do you want to go and change while I sort Sarah's dress out? Just mind the pins."

Without answering as she's already moved on to Sarah, I head back into the unisex changing rooms. Each stall is a large room to allow maneuvering when trying on wedding dresses, which is what Callie and Thalia are doing right now. Thalia already has her dress, but she's helping Callie who is beside herself with Reece asking her to get married this weekend with Jack and Thalia.

I'm really happy for my big brother and I love Callie. She's so good for him.

Before entering the stall where I've left my clothes, I stand in front of the mirror again unable to get how I look out of my head. Really taking notice of myself like this isn't something that I tend to do. I like dressing up, but prefer jeans and shirts.

"Beautiful," I hear from behind me.

Looking up, my eyes meet Donovan's through the mirror. He's standing not too far behind me in a tux and he takes my breath away.

I turn. "Handsome," I counter as I feel his eyes caressing me.

Donovan walks closer and stands directly in front of me. Brushing a piece of hair behind my ear, I tingle when his fingers touch my lobe. My nipples have started to throb with his closeness and his touch. All he has to do is look down and he'll know my body wants him. If he looks into my eyes he'll know how much my heart wants him. I'm not hiding anything from him again. My want of him is clear as day. He can see it easily if he so chooses.

He reaches out and caresses my lily tattoo on my shoulder with his finger, bringing me out in goose bumps. And yeah, he notices my arousal. His eyes widen before meeting my gaze. His eyes are now filled with lust, and something more.

"Mara," he whispers, his voice husky. "This is wrong," he says as his face is coming closer and closer to mine.

Anticipating his kiss, my heart thuds in my chest as my female parts sit up and take notice that I'm about to experience my first real kiss from Donovan, but at the last minute he drops his mouth to my neck. His hands land on my hips as he brings me closer to him so I'm in no doubt about how much he wants me.

He keeps his face buried in the crook of my neck where it meets my shoulder. His mouth opens and I briefly feel his tongue against me as his hands tighten on my hips. Then he starts placing kisses along my shoulder.

My fingers slide through his hair, holding him to me as I feel his cock surge against me through our clothing. I should be frightened feeling how big he is, but I'm not—I'm excited.

Before I'm ready, I feel him pulling back—reining in his passion for me. He keeps his mouth and hands on me, but pulls me into him for a hug. One of his hands slides up my spine to cup my neck, as his other hand holds my head against him. He kisses me on the top of my head and just breathes.

I've never been held like this before. If he completely pushes me away right now, I'm not sure I'm going to handle it well. He's making me feel cherished.

"What are you doing after this?"

Is he going to ask me to spend time with him? Only one-way to find out so I reply, "I don't have anything planned."

"Can you meet me at my place in an hour?" he mumbles into my hair.

"Yes."

Then he slowly starts stepping away from me—reluctantly—before he wraps my hand in his.

"I'll see you in an hour." He kisses my hand before letting me go completely. "Wear jeans and sneakers or something secure on your feet." He blows me a kiss and walks into one of the stalls.

I quickly turn and push into the one I'm using. Locking the door, I turn and rest my back against it with my hand going to my heart. If I hadn't already lost my heart to him, I would have now.

My pulse is frantic—I'm finding it difficult to breathe. I've longed for him to look at me the way he just did—to have him hold me in his arms without it being sexual. I know we were both aroused, but the embrace said more to me than words. There isn't any way that Sarah will affect him the way I think that I do. My only hope is that, in the long run, she won't be a bitch over Donovan.

Out of all my sisters, she's the one that I don't get on with that well. We can usually put up with each other for short lengths of time, but days on end we'd probably murder each other. Despite the fact that we can't always get along, she's still my sister and I love her.

Sighing, I struggle out of the dress with only a few scratches from the pins. Hanging it up, I quickly dress with my heart full of excitement as I wonder what he has planned for us this afternoon. I also can't help wondering why he's decided to will-ingly spend time with me.

"Mara, what are you doing in there?"

I roll my eyes hearing Amanda—if I'm close to any of my sisters then it's Amanda. My younger sis-ters piss me off—always pinching my things and wearing my clothes. At least, they did wear my clothes until my hips got more of a curve and my chest expanded. Basically my body saved my wardrobe.

"I'm ready," I call slipping my feet into my boots.

Grabbing my phone, I pluck the dress from the rack and take it out to the show room to put it on the rack with the dresses for the rehearsal dinner. This is just too weird—two weddings together. Two best friends marrying best friends. *Cute.*

Seeing Callie with a dreamy look on her face, I go over and hug her. "How you doing?"

She laughs. "I think I'm still in shock. But I'm really happy Mara. I'm happier than I've ever been. Your brother is one of the good guys, and I can't wait to be his wife."

"You're good for him." I smile.

"And what about you Mara? Are you happy?" she asks tilting her head to the side as she watches me, waiting for my answer.

"I'm happy." I'm actually giddy with excitement, which is becoming difficult to conceal.

"Hmm. Just be careful," she covers my mouth with her hand, "with him. I know Mara. I caught what happened not too long ago in there." She smiles. "Shit, you both got me all hot and bothered. How long has this been going on?"

"There isn't anything going on. At least not yet, and don't worry I'm conscience of Reece's feelings on the subject—all the time."

She chuckles.

"Just be careful and watch your back," she whispers as Sarah and Amanda join us. "I'll catch you in a bit."

"Okay."

"What were you two whispering about?" Amanda asks, while Sarah watches me with distrust clear in her eyes.

"Weddings." I start to edge toward the door. "I'll see y'all later."

Quickly walking to the new Starbucks store that opened about six months ago, I feel their eyes on me. And then laugh out loud at how absurd I'm being. I can feel them watching me after my hasty departure, but there isn't anything sinister going on. God, I read too many books.

9

DONOVAN

I'M NOT SURE WHAT I'M DOING RIGHT NOW. Seeing Mara looking so beautiful in her dress did something to me. I've never seen anyone as beautiful and I knew I needed to see where this thing between us is going. Reece is going to be a problem, but for now, we can keep it quiet, and just enjoy our day together. At least I hope that's what we can do, or rather, I hope that's what she wants to do.

I hadn't missed the looks Sarah was throwing in my direction as I excused myself from the store earlier. No sooner had I pulled up back here than I had a text message from her asking about my plans for the rest of the day. I decided to ignore her. Constantly replying is keeping her texting me, which I can do without.

Hearing footsteps, I stick my head out of the window and smile as I watch Mara walk toward me, unaware she's being watched. She's beautiful with a head of thick dark curls, which are bouncing as she walks. Having my hands tangled in the silken strands back at the store was heaven and hell. I really didn't want to leave her or rather I wanted to drag her back into the stall with me to see what she was wearing beneath the dress. It had become obvious that she wasn't wearing a bra as I remember her nipples pushing, large and prominent, against the thin fabric of her dress. As she gets closer, I rearrange my dick to a more comfortable position and try to get my brain focused on something other than Mara's delicious body.

I'm not too sure what I want to spend the day doing that involves keeping our clothes on, but when she was in my arms, I knew that I had to have her close again.

I'm so messed up about her. I'm even worried about the state of my house. I've spent the past hour making sure my house is tidy and that I haven't left any dirty laundry lying around—first impressions and all that. Mara's been inside my home more times than I can count, but this is the first time I've invited her here to spend time with me.

Inhaling, I run to the back porch just in time to

watch her walk up the steps. When she spots me, her whole face lights up.

"Hi," she says, looking shy. "Um, Donovan."

"Shit. Sorry. You're here." My befuddled brain is refusing to work and instead of acting cool, I'm acting like an idiot. "C'mon in." I hold the door open for her and catch a hint of her strawberry scent as she passes me. "Can I get you a cold drink," I ask over my shoulder as I walk into the kitchen space.

"That would be good. You've kept the place up. It's just as it always was."

As she takes the drink I pass to her, I shove my hands into the back of the jeans so I don't reach for her. "It's the same, but no baking smells. Let's go out on the porch."

Mara sits in the chair Jack has a habit of using, before kicking off her boots and curling her feet underneath her. What I wouldn't give to have the right to go to her, pick her up from the chair and sit in it myself before settling her in my lap.

"You're staring."

I drop into my seat and grin at her. "I was. I can't stop."

She returns my grin. "I don't mind, really. So what do you have planned?"

Sitting forward with my arms resting on my

knees, I chuckle and admit, "I don't really have any plans. I thought we could get my bike out and go for a ride, but I'm not sure where. To be honest, I just want to spend some time with you." I watch her through half-lidded eyes and her eyes glow back at me. She likes hearing that.

"I'd spend all my time with you, Donovan, if I could, and I think you know that."

I nod in acknowledgement.

"You want to take the bike out with me? Go to Orange Beach."

"Orange Beach? That's just over an hour away."

"I know."

Hours of having her wrapped around my back sounds like heaven—her legs rubbing against mine —*torture*.

"I don't have any beach stuff with me."

Shaking my head, I get to my feet. "C'mon. I think Callie left some clothes the last time she stayed here with Reece. She probably has a bikini or something."

Mara slides her hand into mine so I tighten my fingers around hers. Keeping her with me as we walk through the house to the spare bedroom that Reece uses when he stays here, I enjoy the feeling of her with me.

At least with Callie having been here with him,

the room is neat, which is a huge change from the slob Reece can be.

"She said she was leaving stuff in the top drawer so check in there." I point to the set of drawers to the right of the bed. And feel her loss when she removes her hand from mine.

Sitting on the bed for want of something to do, I watch as she opens the drawer and roots around before pulling out a string bikini.

Oh hell no!

"This is nice," she says, holding the bikini up before stretching the cups of the top apart.

There isn't anyway she's wearing that scrap of material. I'll be fighting every fucker off, not to mention I'll be walking around with a permanent hard-on.

She tosses the bikini panties down on top of the set of drawers, before holding a triangle of material up to her left breast. All it's going to cover is a nipple at this rate. What the hell was I thinking? Not that I spend any time thinking about Callie's attributes, but I guess she is smaller than Mara.

Then she glances at me, and smiles, saying, "This will do," before sauntering out of the bedroom.

I'm left with a hard-on ready to pound nails. I'm

not going to survive today watching her walk around in that thing Callie calls a bikini.

Needing a minute, I make sure my tee shirt covers what's going on in my jeans before heading toward my room. "I'll be out in a minute. Just grabbing some shorts."

Closing my bedroom door, I make quick work of getting my jeans off, following them with my shorts as my dick springs free and jerks as the air hits it. The tip is wet with excitement, but it's going to have to behave for now. I don't have time to stroke one off, although I'd probably last all of thirty seconds right about now.

Opening my closet, I grab a pair of swim shorts and yank them up my legs in frustration—sucking in a breath when I brush against my dick. I'm going to have a bad case of blue balls by the time today is over with.

Grabbing my jeans, I shove my legs back into them while praying for strength. I might have had my eyes open to her a couple of years back, but never have I struggled to control myself around her. It's as though now she's turned eighteen all the hands off signs are gone. I'm ignoring Reece for now because for the first time since my parents died, I want something for me. She makes me feel alive rather than stuck in a rut and I really need that right now.

Hearing my phone beep with a text, I'm pulled out of my thoughts about the girl waiting out on the porch for me. I palm my phone and watch her leaning over the railing, as she looks lost in thought, staring at the lake.

With a quick glance, I cuss. *Sarah*—again!

"Is everything okay?"

"Um, yeah. It's fine." I slip my phone into my back pocket and walk toward her. "Are you ready to go?"

"I am. I've changed into the bikini, and I've put two towels into the knapsack that I found by the door." She hauls it up into her arms. "But we could do with some sunscreen."

"I'll go grab it. We can get drinks when we get there," I add as I reach up into the cupboard for the high factor sunscreen.

I wonder if she'll need help rubbing it on. Okay, perhaps I better not go there.

"I think that's everything." I pass the sunscreen to her before getting my keys for the garage and bike off the hook. "Let's go."

10

MARA

Slipping out of my jeans, I fold them neatly and put them into the knapsack we brought with us. I'll keep my shirt on for now until I can work up the courage to practically bare all. I might wait until Donovan gets back so I don't miss his reaction.

On arriving, because we'd been on Donovan's bike, we'd managed to park directly at the footpath leading to the sand and ocean. It really is beautiful here. Sitting for over an hour on the back of his bike wasn't exactly comfortable, although it was exhilarating. Not just the fresh air on my face filled with the heat you always get during our Alabama summer, but because I had an excuse to put my hands on Donovan. I didn't miss the hiss that escaped his lips as soon as I'd climbed on the bike behind him, or the shudder that had rippled across his body as I slipped my hands around his stomach and slid my thighs against his.

Smiling, I re-arrange the umbrella he bought so it covers the knapsack, leaving room for the drinks Donovan has gone to purchase from the beach café. About to get comfortable on the towel, I remember that I haven't put any sunscreen on yet so bending down I root through the bag, which is how Donovan catches me.

"What the fuck!"

I spin around, nearly toppling over. Donovan stops me from landing on my ass by grabbing hold of my arm. "What?"

"Sorry. I didn't mean to frighten you. But, well, never mind."

Hiding my smile, I make sure I'm facing him as I peel my tee shirt off.

"Jesus, Mara," he cusses in a strangled voice as my head appears from beneath the clothing.

I toss my shirt on top of the bag and look at him. He has a flush along his strong cheekbones and just before he turns away from me, I catch the bulge behind his zipper.

"You must be hot in your jeans. Didn't you put swim shorts on before we left?"

"Yeah. I'm fine for now" He glances at me from over his shoulder. "Are you sure you want to wear that?" He turns to face me again and stands with his hands on his hips. "We can find you something else. They have wetsuits over there."

Wetsuits? Is he serious?

I glance up at his face and, yeah, he's serious.

"What do I need a wetsuit for?"

"Forget I mentioned it," he says before dropping on to a towel and raising his knees with a wince.

Sitting down next to him, I try to hide my grin because I know exactly what his problem is, and it's all to do with the bikini I'm wearing. I'm practically naked, but if it gets his blood going, I'm not about to change or to act self-conscious. Covering up is my first instinct, but it's not going to happen now I've seen how Donovan reacts to me.

"Donovan don't be stupid, you're going to fry if you keep your jeans on."

Jumping to his feet, he turns away and strips his jeans down his long, muscular legs, with hardly any hair coating them, before dropping back to this towel.

"Happy now?"

"That depends. Are you more comfortable?"

He shakes his head and ignores me, but I catch him watching me out of the corner of his eye while I start smoothing sunscreen on my legs, then my arms before finally settling for my stomach. When I get to my chest, he makes a kind of choking noise before suddenly flipping over and lying on his stomach, looking away from me.

Rolling my eyes, I quickly finish with the sunscreen, but realize I can't reach my back so I settle on my stomach on the towel and whisper, "Um, Donovan."

He groans and turns to look at me. "What, babe?"

I smile at the endearment and ask, "Can you rub the sunscreen into my back for me, please?" knowing how his body is affected by mine.

He's not the only one affected though. My breasts and nipples are aching with arousal, which match the ache going on between my thighs—an ache I haven't felt there before.

"Shit, Mara. Pass me the sun stuff."

I pass it to him and rest my face on my hands before I wiggle into a more comfortable position with my legs slightly partied.

And then I feel the sunscreen hit my back, which causes me to gasp at the coldness on my heated skin, but my gasp turns into a moan as Donovan's hands start to smooth it in along my spine to the edge of the bikini panties before he moves back up to my shoulders. He gentle massages the muscle there and the gentle caress that he's doing is making me feel sleepy. But I'm wide-awake when his hands start to rub my bottom where the panties have ridden up before briefly slipping between my legs. With a mind of their own my legs fall open, desperate for his touch to move higher to my core.

"*Mara,* you're killing me."

Turning my head so I can see him—and see him I do—standing at attention. I lick my lips before meeting his gaze.

"We're on a beach, Mara." He pushes his dick back against his body with his hand. "I'm going to lie in the shade and catch up on some sleep."

He fastens the sunscreen back up and tosses it near to the knapsack before climbing over me with his towel and setting up beneath the sun umbrella.

Lifting up slightly, I grab the wallet that I'd placed slightly beneath the towel before I settled down with my kindle paper white in. I'm half way through reading Butterfly Girl by Rona Jameson.

Donovan is snoring away to my left and in his sleep he's flipped over on to his back. As he snores away, I admire him. He really is a beautiful man with his short dark hair, five o'clock shadow and abs that make my mouth water. Even in sleep I affect him—his dick is pushing up against his shorts—and

74

he's growing. I'm unable to move my eyes away from him.

I wonder what or whom he's dreaming about that has his dick so hard and ready with the slight jerking movements every now and again.

Is it me he's dreaming about?

With watching Donovan's arousal grow, mine is pushing at my body for more, but more what? My nipples are rock hard and every slight movement against the sand causes desire to shoot straight between my legs. I might not have that much experience with guys or how they're supposed to make me feel, but I know there is only one guy my body craves just as much as my heart does.

Should I make the first move? It's been obvious over the past few weeks that he wants me just as much as I want him. Well, I hope he wants me just as much.

I've just never been so forward before, but if I don't do anything, we're both probably going to be ninety by the time he gets around to something else. I loved being close to him in the changing room of the dress store, but I need more now—so does my body.

Slowly, so as not to wake him, I crawl closer and cuddle in to his side. His sleepy eyes open then widen when he realizes I'm in his arms and that my hand is caressing over his stomach. He stops my wandering hand with his.

"What are you doing? On a beach, in public."

"I have an ache," I blurt out, raising one leg over his. I bend my knee and nudge against his erection with it.

He groans and closes his eyes.

"We are not doing this." He rolls on top of me, pinning me beneath him. His cock throbs between my legs. "Jesus, Mara." His forehead drops to mine. "We can't," he whispers as his mouth is slowly getting closer and closer to mine.

"Kiss her dude," someone shouts, breaking the spell.

"Yeah, go on kiss her."

Donovan turns his head to the sound of voices, and starts grinning like an idiot. I look as well and start laughing. There are about eight guys, around the same age as me, standing not too far away staring at us.

With a bow, they leave us alone.

"Just in time," Donovan comments, kneeling up between my thighs. Swiping a hand across his face, he says, "I want you Mara, you know that, but you really need to stop teasing me."

Okay, now I'm getting angry. Why does he have to act like it's my entire fault that he wants me? I know I've been teasing him this afternoon, but he's acting as though he had nothing to do with his body's reaction. *Dick!*

Shoving him over on his ass, I get to my feet and grabbing my floppy, white sunhat with a sunflower on that he bought me when we arrived, I ignore him and stride to the ocean to calm down.

I hate this between us. I also hate the fact that my idiot of a brother is in the middle. If it wasn't for him.

"Mara, wait up," Donovan shouts, breaking into my thoughts.

I slow my step, but not altogether and wait for him to catch up to me when I reach the ocean.

11

DONOVAN

Catching up to Mara, I've no idea what to say to her. She's standing in front of me looking so damn hot, and I don't just mean from the heat. The sun seems to shimmer on her body and the way she fills out Callie's bikini should be illegal.

Shaking my head of the lustful thoughts that got me into this to begin with, I reach for her hand and entwine my fingers with hers.

"I'm not sure what happened back there," I admit, hoping she isn't going to get mad all over again. "I'm presuming it was something I said, but—"

"I felt as though you were blaming me for the way your body reacts to me." She faces the ocean. "All I want is for you to want me as much as I want you," she whispers, close to tears.

My heart misses a beat or two in my chest while it registers what she's just admitted. I use my other hand and tilt her face up to me instead of the ocean so I can press a quick kiss to her lips. Nothing like I actually want to do, but better than nothing at all.

Feeling the ocean lap around my ankles, I hold her gaze. "I want you more than you'll ever know— probably more than you want me, but you're my best friend's little sister. Reece knows me really well, and, him and Jack are the only family I have left. I can't lose that." She goes to pull free of my hand, but I hold tight. "For the first time since college I want to spend time with a girl and for it not to involve sex." I grin. "Even though that's constantly on my mind when I'm with you or not with you. So 24/7 really."

She chuckles, which is what I intended even though it's probably the truth.

"You really are a temptation when fully clothed so imagine what you do to me dressed like this. Or what it does to me knowing all the guys on the beach are ogling my girl."

The smile she gives me lights up her whole face at my words. I don't say anything else not wanting to go into further explanation on the '*my girl.*'

"Let's go in the water."

Tugging on my hand, she pulls me with her into the surf.

Being here with her today is the first time I've been back since my parents passed away. They used to bring me here as a young boy for a few days break here and there. Sometimes, as I got older, they'd bring Reece and Jack with us as well. Fun times.

"Hey, where did you go?" Mara asks, reaching up with her hand to push my hair back from my eyes.

"Thinking." Regardless of what I said five minutes ago, I tug her into my arms with her back against my chest. I wrap my arms around her waist while nuzzling into her neck.

With memory's running through my mind, I need her in my arms to keep me grounded and in the present. It's so easy to go back there when I'm alone.

Hugging is fine though. Right? It's not sexual. At least, not yet it isn't. We need to talk about something to get my mind off my dick and what it wants to do to the girl in my arms. But about what? Ah, I know.

"I need a distraction," I whisper into her ear and feel her shiver against me as I move us into deeper water. "Will you tell me about your blog?"

Although she's standing still, I feel the air around us freeze. Of course she had no idea that I know about her sideline hobby or business, which is surprising, considering how popular it is. About eight months ago I created a new email account so I could follow her blog without her being any the wiser. I also wanted to keep an eye on her—too many fuckers out there.

"How," she clears her throat. "How do you know about that?"

I kiss her shoulder, and tighten my hold around her waist as a more powerful wave moves us with the force of it. The water is now lapping at Mara's chest, cushioning and caressing her breasts. I'm unable to move my eyes from the sight, but as my dick makes itself known, I raise my head from watching over her shoulders and look out to sea as I reply, "I found it by accident."

"Seriously?"

Laughing, I admit, "Well it depends on which way you look at it."

She smacks me on the arm and tries to break free, but I won't let her. "Simmer down, babe. I haven't told anyone if that's what you're worried about. And to put your mind at rest I only know because I was on my way to the back of your house one time and overheard you on the phone. Your voice may have stopped me in my tracks for a few minutes and I overheard what you were saying. Although most of it didn't register until about half way through."

"So you spied on me? Is that what you're saying?" She wiggles round to face me, her hands caressing back and forth on my arms. My hands are now resting on her hips, and as she moves closer there's no hiding my erection.

"Not exactly, um—" What was I about to say? My brain doesn't seem to be working with the waves pushing her against me—her rock hard nipples, rubbing against my chest—my cock rubbing against her stomach.

Closing my eyes, I try to count to ten to get rid of the lust clouding by brain, and the sensations running through my body. But opening my eyes, I see the same desire reflected back at me through Mara's eyes.

Grinding my molars, I close my eyes again and turn her back around and I practically beg her, "Talk to me, Mara. Please distract me." I hiss when her bottom rubs against my balls.

She chuckles and starts talking, "My blog, hmm. I love what I have with Mara's Thoughts. It isn't a very original name, but no one else in my family has any interest in art so it isn't likely they'd find it. When I started writing my reviews for the art books, I never in a million years expected to have such a huge following. Sometimes, I just sit staring at the numbers thinking next time I blink I won't have any and that I'll wake up only to find it's all been a dream. I've always had my nose stuck in books—fiction—non-fiction—about art."

"I remember in the summers you'd be lying in your mom's hammock on the back porch with a book under your nose."

"That was the best. I still do that. Robin insists I'd spend my life lying out back either reading or watching the sky. Out of all my sisters, I think she really gets me. Amanda just stays silent and goes along with everyone. Jessie is too hung up on being a silly teenager and she is too busy going after boys with her friends to notice anything at home. And well, Sarah, you know we don't really get on all that well." She shrugs. "But my blog is all mine and the contacts I've made through it will be approachable for after I've finished my art degree. I'm not a hundred percent sure where I want to specialize yet, which is frustrating—not just for me but my art tutor as well."

"You'll be amazing no matter what direction you choose to follow."

I kiss her on the head and continue to look out

at sea, following a yacht on the horizon before it disappears from sight.

I love Orange Beach at this time of year. The kids are still in school, students are still in college, which leaves the beach for visitors or locals. During the height of summer, some cool parties are held here, which I've been to in the past with the guys. But nothing has ever felt so right than being here with Mara—having her in my arms. *My Sweet Mara.*

"Why don't you put all your college work to use?" She squeezes my arms. "Not that you working at the bar doesn't mean anything, but all that studying and good grades."

Sighing, I admit, "After my parents died I lost interest in so many things, that being one of them. My law degree is still there, but now I've had lots of time to think about it, and my life, I'm not sure that's what I want to do anymore. In fact, I know it isn't. It's just hard admitting that. My father wanted me to follow in his footsteps, and he was beside himself when I told him that I wanted to study law at college. What I didn't admit was that I was choosing that because Jack was. He probably worked it out, but he let it lie because it's what he wanted."

"What did you want to do?"

"Play ball."

She starts laughing.

"Hey! Isn't that what every boy wants to do? Play ball."

"I guess," she agrees still chuckling.

"Okay, seriously, I've always been interested in architecture, but more to do with the exterior than the interior. I've been sketching for years so it's not as though I'm new to it all, but there's a lot to learn."

Going still in my arms, her gaze searches the horizon and I can't help but search it as well as though the answers to the future are on it. She squeezes my arm in a hug and then murmurs, "Let's go back in, I'm getting thirsty."

Without another thought, I head back toward the beach with Mara still in my arms.

"You're back to studying again?" she asks.

I'd thought our conversation was over. In fact, I hoped that would be the end of it. It isn't something I've talked about with anyone before. So it feels weird as I answer her, "Yeah, I am—only this past month though. I signed on for some online courses so I can to see what they're like—if I can handle them with work, so far so good."

Out of the ocean, I let her slip out of my arms

and take hold of her hand, entwining our fingers together. No matter what my body is telling me, I'm not ready to take this, whatever it is, any further. Keeping her close and holding her hand should satisfy me for now. *I hope!*

12

MARA

"Mara, are you asleep?"

"Nearly." I pry my eyes open and watch as Donovan walks closer to where I'm lying in his hammock. On arriving back at his place, we hauled it out from his basement and put it together, which we finished about five minutes ago.

"Are you going to let me share it with you?" he asks with a slight smile on his lips.

"Since it's yours I can hardly refuse," I smile, "but even if it wasn't I'd still move over."

"Okay. Hold on."

I grip part of the hammock and hope Donovan doesn't send me to the floor, but with one quick move it's all sorted and he's tight against me.

"Turn slowly and let me hold you," he offers.

Whom I to refuse a husky request or an excuse to be close to this man? Doing as he asked, I turn and end up half on top of him with his arm around my shoulders holding me tight. My left leg is bent at the knee, resting close to his groin, but he doesn't seem bothered. Snuggling deeper into him, I wrap my arm around his waist and sigh. I want to stay like this forever.

"Hey, you really are tired. Do you want me to take you home?"

"Nope. I'm staying here with you," I slur with sleep pulling me under.

Donovan sighs, "I'd like that, Mara," he starts to weave his fingers through my hair, "but—"

"I can't," I finish his sentence for him.

"Mara." He turns on his side so we're now lying chest-to-chest, hips-to-hips. I slip my knee between his legs and move closer to him, watching him gulp as I do.

"Please kiss me."

He looks like he wants to do nothing more, but he closes his eyes and inhales.

I know he's told me why he won't, that he's frightened he won't be able to stop, but surely we can control our urges while in the hammock. I mean one false move and we'll both topple to the floor.

"Just a small kiss," I whisper waiting for his eyes

to open, but they stay shut and he still doesn't make any move toward me.

Feeling hurt, I bury my face back into his chest as the tears I've been trying to hold at bay trickle from my eyes and on to his tee shirt. I'm not usually so emotional, but around him I obviously am.

"Babe?" he questions, putting me slightly away from him and taking my face in his hands. "Please don't cry. We shouldn't have spent the day together. We shouldn't be lying here together not wanting to leave the other but we have and we are."

Finally!

He leans in and kisses along the trail of tears on my face before he kisses each eye in turn. The kisses don't stop, he moves back down my cheeks and starts to kiss the side of my neck as my hands come up and slide into his hair to hold his head in position. As he starts to nibble along my jaw, I tilt my head slightly and find his lips hovering above mine.

"I can't ask again," I say in a broken voice.

"You don't need to. This was inevitable." He breathes the statement like it's a love poem before gently caressing back and forth against my waiting lips with his. All the while his eyes stay locked on mine. "I'm going to deepen the kiss."

I've never wanted anything as much as I want

his lips on me right now. All day we've been teasing each other and now it's about to become a reality.

His lips are warm and smooth as they finally make contact with mine. My heart is pounding in my chest as he takes his time, placing small kisses along my lips before I feel his tongue pushing between them. Opening my mouth to him, he groans and finally seals his lips with mine. At first his tongue strokes mine in a light, teasing caress then when I press harder against his groin—his dick hard and swollen with his arousal—he deepens the kiss. Our tongues tangle, tasting the other. I'll never get enough of this man.

My hips are grinding against the solid length of him while he ravishes me with his mouth. My hand slips from the back of his head to his waist before dipping over his butt, which I squeeze, pulling him against me.

The ache between my legs intensifies. The more he kisses me—the more I grind against him. I need him to touch me there to ease me, but then he cups my breast and rubs his thumb over my hardened nipple causing a shudder to run through my body. I break from the kiss and moan, pushing more into his hand. "Don't stop. That feels good."

"God Mara, you'd make a saint lose control."

I chuckle, but gasp when he bends his head and gentle bites down on my nipple.

I'm not going to stop him because I want this. He wants this between us just as much. I move my hand to the front of his jeans and push up and down against him. He growls and rolls us out of the hammock. I land on top of him on the floor, but before I can catch my breath he has me up from the floor and in his arms as he strides toward his bedroom.

"I'm not making love to you tonight. You need slow and romantic for your first time. Not only do I need to buy some condoms, but I'm not going to last long enough to prepare you. We're going to get naked though. I hope that's okay."

Is he for real? "Um, yeah that's okay. I've wanted to see you naked for a long time."

"*Fuck.*"

He tosses me on to his bed, following me down before I get a chance to check out his package.

He unfastens my jeans and shoves them down my legs with my panties, dropping them to the floor. I have no shame and open my legs to give him a teasing look between my thighs. Donovan doesn't move as he stares at my sex, his breathing heavy. Taking hold of my tee shirt, I pull it off over my head and toss it somewhere on the floor, following it with my bra. I'm now completely naked for the only man who makes my heart wild.

"You have too many clothes on," I huskily tell him.

Quickly jumping from the bed, he shucks his clothes in record time and stands before me in his naked glory. He's beautiful. All hardened muscle, not an inch of fat to him. My eyes wander all over him, but they keep straying back to his manhood, which is standing proudly from a light sprinkling of hair.

Not too sure what to do as I've never been naked with anyone before, I move to sit in front of him on the bed. Reaching out, I stroke his shaft with a finger and feel him jerk as he leaks at the tip. I lick my lips. Needing to taste him in the most erotic way a woman can taste a man, I lean closer. Wrapping my hand around him, I swirl my tongue around the head of his cock and hear him cuss above me.

Knowing I affect him as badly as he does me, I move my hand up and down his shaft getting the feel of Donovan's smooth silken length. Dipping my head over him again, I take the head slightly in my mouth and massage him with my tongue. His taste explodes on my tongue, and I can't help feel that bit of rejection that he won't make love to me.

"Mara, *fuck!* You have to stop."

He pulls free of my mouth, and before my disappointment can really take hold, he has me on my back on the bed with him between my spread thighs. He rests his elbows on either side of my chest to keep his weight, which I want, from me. His dick rests against my hip.

"You are so beautiful, Mara. I can't believe it's me you want."

I smile. "I've always wanted you. So believe it, because I'm not going anywhere."

"No, you're not."

He kisses me on the nose before grinning and sliding down my body. With a suck and nibble to each of my breasts, he moves further south and starts to kiss his way down past my navel to the strip of hair I have on my pussy. But he doesn't stop there and using his fingers, he spreads me open before dipping his tongue in.

The pleasure that shoots through my body has me throwing my head back as I grip the covers beneath me, arching my hips into his mouth. Whatever he's doing to me is driving my body higher and higher. My pussy keeps clenching and releasing around his finger, but I want—need—more. I need him. Over me. Inside me.

"Donovan," I moan. "Come here please."

He stops and looks up from between my legs, his mouth wet.

"You taste good, baby." He licks his lips.

Reaching out with my arms, he realizes that I want him to come up to me. He wraps his arms around me and holds me tight with his balls wedged against me.

I wrap my legs around his thighs, and moving against him, I feel an orgasm starting to build.

My breathing is uneven as I dig my fingers into his butt to push him down on me. I need something. I need Donovan.

He takes my mouth in a bruising kiss as he pushes hard against where I need him, and I lose all control of my body as I start to convulse in a mind-numbing climax—flooding his balls with my release. I can't stop. My climax is going on and on. I vaguely hear Donovan groan before I feel his dick twitching between us before a new wetness follows.

Eventually we both slow down and come to a stop, breathing heavily against the other. Donovan lifts his head and places a sweet kiss to my lips. "I need to clean you up." He raises himself off me and kneels between my spread thighs. "I'm sorry."

What the hell!

I can't stop the tears that gather in my eyes at his apology for this.

"Shit, Mara. Don't cry. I'm apologizing for coming all over you," he says sheepishly. "That wasn't supposed to happen. I wanted this to be about you, not me. It's just, I've wanted you for so damn long. You had me really worked up, and then when you came all over my balls, I lost it."

"So you're not sorry for having me naked and beneath you?"

"Fuck, no!"

He looms over me. "I should be bothered about this whole situation, but I'm not going there right now because you're with me so I'm happy. I hope you are as well."

"I am."

"Good. I think the quickest way to get cleaned up is a shower, although I'm not sure I'm going to survive seeing your naked body covered in shower gel."

He leans down and scoops me up in his arms.

"Maybe I could rub the shower gel on you. I mean to make sure you're clean and all," I say, knowing exactly what I'm doing to him.

13

DONOVAN

MAKING BREAKFAST FOR THE GIRL IN MY BED IS a first. I'd slept all night with my girl wrapped up in my arms. It had felt like the most natural thing in the world to have her with me. Despite my history as a player, she is the only girl to have stepped foot in my bedroom. Hell, she's the first girl I've ever brought to this house. Usually I'd go to their place so I could leave as soon as the deed was done. Quick escape. But last night after we'd showered and given each other another orgasm, I'd asked her to stay the night. The smile I'd received in response to those words had made me feel on top of the world.

Who knew that having the girl of my dreams come all over my balls could be so damn satisfying. From the moment she touched my cock with a tentative stroke I'd been ready to explode with excitement. If I had the chance to slide into her virgin sheath I'd probably come before hitting her barrier.

Groaning, I reach out to the counter with my hands and rest against it, breathing heavily. As I look down, my arousal is tenting my sweat pants.

Lost in my thoughts and lust, I don't hear Mara sneak up on me, but I sure as hell feel her as she presses her naked front against my back and wraps her arms around my waist. Her hand wanders down and finds me hard and ready for round three.

"Mmm, someone is excited to see me."

Laughing, which turns into a groan as she wraps her hand around me, I admit, "I'm always happy to see you, and I don't just mean what's going on in my sweats."

I feel her smile against me. "I know."

She kisses me on the back before quickly getting on her knees between me and the kitchen cabinets. Before my brain can catch up she has my sweats around my ankles and her hand around my cock. I don't even get a chance to catch my breath before she's sucking me into her wet mouth—her hot, tight mouth. *Fuck.*

My legs quiver so I grip the counter even harder to try and keep myself upright as she starts to massage my balls while creating a delicious, toe curling suction along my length. My cock swells as she sucks and licks at me.

God, nothing has ever felt as good. I've been blown before, too many times to count, but it has never felt like an all-consuming volcano is ready to detonate from my balls out of my dick.

Then the warmth has gone, but she wraps her mouth around me and licks down to my balls before sucking each one, in turn into her mouth for a quick massage. Wrapping her hand around the base of me, she licks back up to my leaking tip, and swirls her tongue around, lapping at all the pre-cum running out of me. I can't control it.

"I'm going to come—soon—oh God, Mara."

She sucks me straight back into her mouth at the same time as she massages my balls, and then I feel it—the spark at the base of my spine—the fire in my balls. I ignite and come as she continues to swallow and suck around me. *Heaven!*

Lapping me up, she licks all around my shrinking cock before releasing me, and I do what any guy would do after such a mind-numbing blow, and slide to the floor with sweats still around my ankles.

She giggles and climbs astride me, wrapping her arms around my neck. My arms go around her, pulling her tight against my chest.

Kissing her messy locks, I say the only words that come to mind, "Thank you." Then add, "Let me rest a few more minutes then I'm going to return the favor."

"No, you're not. That was all for you. If you return the favor then it takes away from the gift I've just given you."

"Um, wow." She blows my mind, and I will be returning the favor, just not this morning. Although I'd love to taste her again, I'm not a dick and don't want to spoil what she's just done for me so unselfishly.

"Cat got your tongue?"

"That was. I've never. Fuck," I laugh, "I can't even string a sentence together."

"That good, huh?"

"Yeah."

"We need to buy condoms," she says, kissing up my neck.

"We do?"

"Yes. I want to feel you inside me. I want to know what it feels like to come with your hard and thick dick massaging my walls while I do."

"Fuck, Mara," I growl.

Chuckling, she gives me a quick peck to my check before sliding to the side of me. Before she can play again, I quickly grab my sweats and pull them up, covering my hardening problem.

"I was going to bring you breakfast in bed, but as you're up, please put some clothes—"

"Donovan, you up yet?"

My eyes meet Mara's.

Fuck.

"Donovan?" Jack shouts again.

We're screwed, more so if Reece is with him.

There's no way Mara can get back to the bedroom without being seen, plus she's naked and I sure as hell don't want him getting a glimpse of my naked girl.

He needs to stay where he is.

Placing my finger across my lips so Mara knows I want her to stay quiet, I jump up from the floor and greet a startled Jack.

"What the fuck. Wait a minute. You have someone with you as in behind the cabinets?"

There isn't anyway to get out of this so I might as well be upfront with him and hope he doesn't inform Reece before I get the chance. No matter how badly I think Reece will take me being with his sister, he still needs to hear it from me. Keeping it to ourselves isn't really an option, plus now that I have Mara I'm not willing to keep her a secret.

"Pass me that shirt." I point to the one on top of

my clean laundry so at least I can get her covered up first.

Catching the tossed shirt, I pass it to Mara and when she's covered I take her hand and pull her up, and into my side.

Jack doesn't say anything, he just stands there. His mouth opens and shuts and his eyes glaze over like he's in a trance. A wry smile twists the corner of his lips as he stares between the two of us.

"This is bad," he finally says. "Reece is going to go off when he finds out about the two of you. You know that right? *Fuck!* This is going to screw up the wedding."

"How the hell is me being with Donovan going to screw up your wedding?" Mara asks what I'm thinking.

"Are you fuckin' with me right now? It's only a few days before the wedding and Reece is going to go crazy when this," he waves his hand between us, "comes to light."

"Look, I'll tell Reece myself. I'm not ashamed to be with Mara. I'm also not willing to push her away because her brother doesn't agree with us being together. She's changed me. I only want her."

I tighten my arm around her.

"Since when do you do virgins?"

What the fuck!

"You're one of my best friends Jack, but I'm not going to stand here and listen to you talk about her like that. It's no one's business."

"I'm still a virgin," Mara announces before burying her head in my chest.

I can't help but grin when I see Jack imitating a fish.

"I mean. What the hell have you two been doing if you're still one of them?" he asks wincing.

"Lots. Why are you here so early?"

He gets comfortable on one of the chairs and after swiping his hand down his face, drops his head back and answers me, "Reece has been trying to call you," he says, turning to glare at me, "so here I am. Just be glad it was me and not him. You need to tell him so he doesn't catch you like I have."

I whisper to Mara, "Go put some clothes on babe." I clench my fists to my side to refrain from smacking her on the ass as I watch her leave.

I walk into the living room and slide into the chair opposite Jack. I watch as a shit-eating-grin spreads across his face.

"I knew it was only a matter of time before the two of you got together. My only hope was that Reece would have loosened up some beforehand."

"Reece is never going to loosen up where Mara is concerned. He has five sisters, well six, if you count Dahlia, and it would just be my luck that he's closest to Mara."

Jack throws his head back and roars with laughter.

That's how Mara catches us. "Well you two look to be having fun."

"Come here, babe."

She's wearing her jeans from yesterday and looks to have borrowed my baseball jersey.

Climbing onto my lap, she snuggles against me as my arms wrap around her, keeping her close.

"Like the shirt," I comment, and she smiles.

"Well, one things for sure," we turn our heads to look at Jack as he continues, "you only have to look at you to see the difference between before and now. I hope Reece sees what I do."

Jack stands and starts heading toward the door. "Oh," he does an about turn, "Reece wanted you to swing by the wedding shop and pick up your tux, which is ready. Also, the rehearsal dinner has been confirmed at the country club. It starts at seven *sharp* on Friday. Mara, you'll need to be there as well."

"Of course she's going to be there. Why wouldn't she?" Now I'm confused. She'd be there regardless, but I'd want her with me as my guest otherwise.

"This thing between the two of you isn't going to go down too well with her family, not just Reece. You need to consider that before you let the world know what's going on before the wedding."

"You want us to stay quiet until after the wedding? That's what you're trying to tell me?"

"It might save a lot of stress if Reece and Callie don't find out until afterwards. We're going away for a few days after the wedding so, hopefully, by the time we get back and Reece finds out, he'll be too mellow to really get into it with you."

Mara laughs. "My brother is going to get into it with us regardless of how much sex he's had before hand, and you know that. I'm Donovan's date for my brother's wedding."

"You are," I blurt out before censoring my response.

"Of course I am because I'd seriously have to kill anyone else you took." She grins at me.

"You have your hands full. I'm gonna get back to my girl." Jack smiles and opens the door. I can hear him whistling the tune of Jaws as he leaves and I know he's expecting the shark, Reece, to tear me a new one.

Mara straddles my lap.

"I am going with you right?" she asks while chewing on her bottom lip.

"Babe, we're both in the wedding party so we're both going to be there anyway. We will also be sitting with everyone, but yes, you are going to be with me. I just need to figure out the best time to talk to Reece."

"Can we wait until after the wedding just in case he really gets pissed? I mean, Callie won't want wedding pictures with Reece having a black eye, and you for that matter considering you're the best man."

"There isn't going to be a fight."

"Really?" She grins. "You're not telling me that Reece won't go for you when he finds out you de-flowered me."

"I haven't de-flowered you yet."

"I know. Condoms. We need lots of condoms."

"Oh, we do, do we?" I tickle her, which has her squirming around in my lap—not such a good idea. "We can go and get some flavored ones after breakfast."

"Flavored? Why flavored? Oh no. Normal ones will be fine because I have no intention of having any latex between you and my mouth."

"C'mon." I move her from my lap. "Let's get breakfast, otherwise, we'll be going nowhere any time soon."

14

MARA

"WHERE HAVE YOU BEEN? MOM'S BEEN looking for you," Sarah asks, sounding pissed because I stayed out overnight. She hates not knowing what's going on, and heaven forbid if her younger sister has a boyfriend before she does!

"Mom knows exactly where I've been because I sent her a text message last night letting her know, and she replied."

The moment I arrived home, Sarah had accosted me. I hadn't even made it up the steps before she did, but I brushed past her. I knew what she wanted to ask me so I purposely ignored her because it's none of her business. She always makes me feel like everything is a competition with her, and it isn't. Although she's really going to piss me off if she carries on whispering with Amanda about Donovan. Not only will she be putting Amanda on the spot, but if Reece finds out he'll totally flip —maybe.

"What are you doing today?"

So now she's trying the 'let's be friends' tact, which will not work, either.

"I have some studying to do. I'll see you later," I say from halfway up the stairs on my way to my room.

I'm not telling her that I'm only home to change clothes before I sneak out and go and see Bonny over at the doctor's office. Although I better give her a call first to make sure she's working today.

Donovan dropped me off five minutes away from the house so as I walked the rest of the way home, I looked up the contraceptive injection on my phone. It says that it's effective straightaway if you have it within five days of your period. Well, I started with an aching stomach on my way home with Donovan so I figured I'm okay to have it now, which is where Bonny comes in.

She's one of the family planning nurses at the clinic so I'm hoping she'll give me the injection without getting on the phone with my mom the minute I leave, like Suzanna would have done. I've told Bonny things in the past that I don't think she's repeated so I'm going to put my trust in her.

I'd love nothing more than to have sex with Donovan without having anything between us—to feel his silken length as he moves back and forth inside me. I wonder what he'll feel like inside me though. He's big. I know the first time is supposed to hurt, but knowing Donovan, he'll make sure the pain is minimal. Right now, I can honestly say I'm not frightened—more like excited. He makes me feel so special and just being in his presence makes me feel like the luckiest girl in the world.

At the beach yesterday, there had been so many beautiful girls and he never once stared at them. A few had tried to get his attention, but he'd turned to me instead. At least I know where his mind is, or rather whom his mind is on.

Smiling in remembrance, I throw my clothes off and head for another shower before I put some clean ones on.

Stepping under the hot spray, I decide that today feels like a sundress kind of day. Plus if I'm meeting Donovan later then I want to tease him. He can't get in my panties for a few days, and I thank God my periods only usually last around three days. So Thursday, the day before the rehearsal dinner, I should be finished and ready to go. I just need to keep Donovan on pins until then so he doesn't have second thoughts because of my over-bearing brother. Don't get me wrong, I love Reece, but I'm old enough to lead my own life and I wish he'd let me, instead of interfering.

I know he'll eventually come around to me being with Donovan, but to begin with he's going to spit bricks, he'll be so mad. I know the life Donovan's led with Reece before my brother met Callie, so it's not as though I don't know where Reece is coming from. But, I believe Donovan when he says he only wants me. Even Jack believed him.

Stepping out of the shower, I quickly wipe myself dry, and after seeing to my *girl problem,* slip into skimpy yellow panties and one of my new sundresses hanging in my closet. It's lemon cotton with a fitted bodice, spaghetti straps hold it up and a full skirt covers my thighs, with the dress coming to a stop above my knees. It reminds me of the kind of dresses they wore in the fifties. I love it.

Slipping my ballerina pumps on to my feet, I'm tempted to change them out for my Uggs. I love my boots and have a habit of wearing them no matter the weather—even in the Alabama heat.

As I hide behind my curtains the ballerina's are still on my feet while I try to see if anyone is out back. To my delight, Sarah is on the back porch with a couple of her friends. This means, I'll hope-fully, be able to get out of the house without anyone being the wiser. At least that's the plan.

Turning back to my room, I find Amanda standing in the doorway. I hadn't even heard her open the door.

"Can I come in?"

I nod my head and sit on my bed waiting for her to join me.

She doesn't. She hovers near the closed door.

"What's going on?"

"Can't I come in and talk to my sister, who I haven't seen for a few weeks, when I want to?"

Flopping back on to the bed, I pat beside me. Amanda comes and lies next to me.

"What's going on with you and Donovan?"

Wow. Direct.

"What makes you think there's something be-tween me and Donovan?" I counter to try and bide my time because I really don't want to lie out right to her. Despite wanting to, I can't tell her the truth —at least not yet.

"I'm not blind, Mara. No matter what Sarah thinks, he's only ever had eyes for you."

I roll on to my side so I can look into her face. "You're serious. I honestly don't know what to say."

"It's okay. Perhaps it's best if you don't. That

way I won't have to lie to Sarah if she asks me if I know anything. Just be careful, okay? She has this weird notion in her head that it's her he wants when anyone with twenty-twenty vision can see it's you."

"I don't know why she always seems to have it in for me. She's so bad tempered." I flop over on to my back and stare up at the glow in the dark stars on my ceiling. I stuck them up there with Reece about six or seven years ago.

"I don't think she's happy. I think deep down she knows he isn't in to her. She'll get over it. She doesn't really have much choice."

"Let's talk about something else," I'm sick of talking about Sarah, "like you."

She groans.

"I'm boring. You're much more fun or at least you're going to be when Reece finds out Donovan has the hot's for you—and it's returned."

I elbow her in the side. "Stop. I want to hear more about the job you're doing in town."

"It's just at the law office. It gets boring but the scenery is nice."

"Nice? Since when have hot lawyers been 'nice'?"

I watch her blush when I turn my head to look at her.

"He's really cute, but shy with women. He's a damn good lawyer though."

"Why the long face?"

"He always smiles at me and greets me when he gets there in the morning, you know he has good manners. But whenever we pass in the hall or I have to go into his office to give him some notes that I've typed up, he gets nervous and blushes. It was cute but now it's bugging me. I want him to ask me out. I'm not fussy. Coffee would be a start. But I'm getting nowhere fast." She sighs.

Smiling to myself at my eldest sister being in a snit over a lawyer, I feel so happy that she's telling me. This feels good—being needed by one of my sisters.

"If he's shy—"

"I'm not sure he is. Only with me."

"Then you need to get a couple of new shirts with a bit of cleavage and some tighter skirts, and then see how he reacts to the change. Whether he looks or not, I'd still invite him out myself. Just go for it."

She groans. "He might say no."

"He also might say yes."

She goes quiet beside me, and I'm positive that she's considering my words.

"I better get going," I say realizing time is getting late.

"Thanks for the chat. I'm going to drive into town and get some new clothes. It's been a long time since I spent some money."

"Then go for it." *And go get him,* I silently add.

We roll off my bed and Amanda hugs me before leaving me alone. Quickly checking out my window again to make sure Sarah is still distracted, I collect my purse from beneath the dirty clothes, and leave my bedroom as quietly as the door will allow. I make my way downstairs and out of the front door, which has been left open a crack to my advantage. Whenever I sneak out, the front door has a habit of making the loudest noise. *But not this time!*

Hurrying across the road, I slip down the back of the corner house so that I can't be seen walking to the crossroads to get into town. That's the beauty about living so close, you can walk pretty much anywhere you want to go—apart from Donovan's that is.

Donovan's home is part way round the lake, and although it can be walked, it would probably take up a good part of the day to do it.

Arriving at the crossroads, I turn right and start to second-guess myself. What if Donovan doesn't want to have sex with me bareback? I mean he's a guy right? Anything to heighten their own pleasure —he'll be game. *Ugh!*

Lost in my own thoughts, I suddenly notice Donovan driving along beside me.

"Hey, babe. Hop in."

He stops so I can climb into the cab with him.

Grinning, I quickly kiss him before sitting back in my seat and belting up.

"Where you heading?"

Hmm. The truth or not?

The truth. "I'm going to see Bonny."

He sends me a questioning look with a raised eyebrow.

"She's the only one I trust to give me the contraceptive injection without telling anyone."

He brakes hard, throwing an arm out in front of me.

"Sorry. Are you okay?"

"Yeah. I take it you don't agree?"

He switches to the gas and gets us moving again. "I just wasn't expecting that to come out of your mouth." He glances at me. "Are you sure you want to do that? Isn't there side effects with having the injection?"

"There's side effects with every medication on the market. This is no different. It just means we can have sex without any latex between us. I've never been with anyone before and I want to feel every bit of you when you're finally inside me."

"Fuckin' hell, Mara."

He's sweating, and yeah, I glance down and notice the bulge in his jeans. I'm getting to him.

"I've never done it without a condom before."

His admission fills me with joy. "Don't you want to make love to me with skin against skin? I mean, think how sensitive your dick will be when its not squished in a condom."

He growls. "You're killing me, Mara. Please change the subject."

"I will when you answer me."

He flexes his hands around the steering wheel before glancing at me again through the corner of his eye. "Making love to you without any barrier would be amazing, and I'd be honored to do that, but don't think for one minute that after we have, that you can be with anyone else because I won't share you—ever."

What the hell is he on about? When have I ever said I wanted to be with someone else? "When have I ever given you reason to believe I'm going to go from you to someone else? I actually thought we had something special and all I could see was a future with you."

I turn to look out of the window feeling disappointed that he could think I'd consider going from him to someone else. That had never entered my head. I haven't even thought about anyone else.

Donovan pulls over at the back of the clinic, and switching the engine off, he unclips my seat belt. Pulling me into his arms, I resist for a second before I slide into his warmth. There is no fight where Donovan is concerned and I'd go wherever he took me. "I'm sorry, Mara." He kisses me on the top of my head. "I didn't mean you were going to go off with someone else after me, I was just trying to tell you in my stupid way that I'm never going to be able to give you up. That applies regardless of when I make love to you." He brushes the hair back from my face. "Are we good?"

"Yeah, we are."

"You want to go park later," he nibbles along my jaw and neck, "and fool around."

I giggle. "How old are you?"

"Now babe, we've never dated and I intend to rectify that. We'll just have to do it low key for now, and parking with you is on my list of things to do."

"You have a list?" I ask surprised.

"Not really." He grins. "But it sounded good."

I hit him on the chest.

"Now enough talking. Kiss me and go get the jab. Where do they put it anyway?"

Rolling my eyes, I cup his face in my hands and looking into his eyes, I kiss him.

As my tongue tangles with his, I change position and sit astride him, wanting more contact. Now that I've tasted him, he's becoming the air I breathe, and I just can't get enough.

"You better go," he groans as I kiss my way along his jaw and bite down on his earlobe before sucking it into my mouth. He arches into me as his hands slide up my dress to land on my bottom. He grips me in his hands, and starts to rub me against the hardness he has going on in his jeans.

It feels so good. I throw my head back and start to ride him, but as I feel his hands slipping inside my panties it brings me abruptly back down to earth.

"Stop."

He freezes.

"I can't."

He looks stunned, but starts to pull away from my bottom.

"I mean. Oh God, this is embarrassing." I cover my face with my hands as I feel a blush starting to rise up from my neck.

"Mara, you have me worried. What's embarrassing?" He starts to soothe me with small caresses up and down my back.

"Um, you get the jab within five days of your period starting."

He freezes then starts to laugh.

"Fuck, woman. You had me worried. I thought I'd done something wrong. There's nothing embarrassing about being a woman." He kisses me on each hand before pulling them from my face to reveal my fiery cheeks. "You look cute all red."

"You're an ass."

"No I'm not. I'm sweet for telling you not to be embarrassed." He gives me a quick kiss to my lips before opening his door and dropping to the ground with me in his arms. "Now go in there and get sorted out, and I'll see you later." After one last kiss, he passes me my purse, pats me on the butt and shoves me in the direction of the back entrance.

"I'll let you know what happens," I shout over my shoulder.

"You better."

Opening the door, I step inside the air-conditioned corridor and spot Bonny coming out of a room further down. When she looks up and sees me, a frown mars her brow before she walks toward me.

15

DONOVAN

Tux in one hand, I push through the door of the wedding store and walk smack into Reece. My mind has been full of Mara, but as soon as I see him everything flies out leaving me tongue-tied—a first for me.

"What the hell is wrong with you?" he asks sounding pissed.

"Nothing," I say then grin. I'm an idiot. "Okay, nothing much. Just lost in thought."

He laughs. "So who's the girl?"

My heart drops to my feet. "Um, someone I took to the beach yesterday."

Telling him the truth, but being a bit evasive will probably work with him right now while his head is full of Callie and their wedding. "I thought your tux was okay. What are you doing here?"

"Shoes," he grouches.

I laugh. "Were you planning on wearing those?" I point down to his scuffed boots.

"I was, but Callie has other ideas."

"You're a dick if you thought Callie would let you get married in them."

He shakes his head. "Yeah, well, I'm thinking another pair of these instead of shoes. I can cope with a lot but I need something I can feel comfortable in."

Shaking my head, I laugh at him again. He reminds me of the time we all had to get suits when we were about fourteen. Can't remember why right now, but he was the same back then about his footwear. Now we're in our twenties, it's kind of weird for a guy to have a thing about his footwear, right? It certainly is to me.

"I think you'll get away with a new pair of boots. It's probably the wrecked look of those that Callie's opposed to you wearing for your wedding rather than the fact they're boots and not shoes. On that note, I'm going to leave you to get sorted, and I'll catch you later."

Turning, I dash toward my truck, hoping he

doesn't call me back to go in the store with him. I can still feel him staring at my back though.

Hanging the tux up on the handle in the rear of the truck, I climb in and pull out behind the two cars on the main road through town. I wonder if Mara has finished at the clinic and if she's okay.

She'd shocked me when she'd told me where she was heading and why. That had been the last thing I'd expected to come out of her mouth. My dick had also stood up and took notice. *Bareback.* Yeah, it definitely likes that idea. *Down boy!* I grin, and before I know where I'm at, I'm pulling up in front of Mara's house. This is probably a really bad idea, but I need to check on her before I head back to my place. A text message isn't going to cut it.

Stepping out of the truck, I groan when I spot Sarah coming toward me across the lawn. She's a pretty girl, more my age, but she isn't Mara. There's only one of her.

"Hey handsome," Sarah shouts in greeting as she gets closer to the truck.

Reaching into the back of the truck, I pull an art book out of the red paper bag that Julie at the local bookstore wrapped for me. I'd wanted to give it to Mara as a present anyway, but I figure I'm going to need a good excuse to get to Mara right now.

Slamming the door, I turn and face her. "Hi Sarah. How are you doing?"

"All the better for seeing you."

I can handle flirting—I think.

"Good to know. Is Mara around?"

Perhaps that was the wrong thing to ask. I watch as her face changes into a scowl. "What do you want her for?"

"Whatever happened to sisterly love?"

"You didn't answer my question." She stands with her hands on her hips in a 'you're not getting past me' move.

Exasperated, I stand my ground. "Sarah, stop being a brat. I'm here to return a book to Mara. Now is she home or not?"

"I'll give it to her." She reaches out to take the book from me, but I hold tight.

"No can do. I want to ask her something about it as—" my breath catches in my throat as I spot her standing at the front door, "Never mind. I see her."

I quickly walk around a shocked Sarah to get to my girl. Probably the wrong move to make, but even from a distance I can make out that Mara doesn't look too good. Her skin is pale and she has her arms wrapped around her stomach in a protective gesture.

"Mara, what's wrong?" I ask as soon as I reach

hearing distance. I jog up the steps to the porch.

She shakes her head, turns and heads back inside.

I follow her upstairs and into her room, where I close the door behind me and lean against it to stop any unwanted visitors.

"Please talk to me."

She lies down on her bed, before turning away from me.

Fuck the door!

Placing the book on her desk, I walk around the bed and climb on, lying down so I'm face to face with her. I'm not fully settled before she moves into my arms.

I wrap mine around her and pull her in flush against me. "Babe," I whisper into her hair, "you're killing me. Did the injection make you sick?"

She shakes her head.

"Give me something so I can stop freaking out or so I know what I'm freaking out over." I stroke down her back and massage her bottom, which isn't such a good idea. Not only is a flaccid cock good right now, I sure as hell don't want to have to walk out of here with an erection.

"Period pains," she mumbles against my chest.

"Are you serious?"

She nods her head.

"*Fuck,* Mara. You had me worried. I mean period pains obviously make you feel like shit, but, God, I thought it was more serious." I put her slightly away from me so I can see her eyes. "Tell me what to do to help you."

She smiles. "You already are."

Returning her smile, I take advantage and kiss her on the lips. What was supposed to be a quick kiss becomes heated when she opens her mouth to me. One taste is all it takes for me to be desperate for more. Chasing her tongue into her mouth, I deepen the kiss as I roll fully on top of her.

She breaks from the kiss, and nibbles my earlobe. "Mmm. That feels good. The pressure on my stomach is easing the pain."

Our mouths meet again and my cock surges with lust when she wraps her legs around my hips, pressing me down into her. Her hands slide into my hair, holding me against her mouth. There isn't any need for that because I've no wish to go anywhere else. I'm in heaven right here with her surrounding me—grinding against my throbbing dick.

Our mouths separate, trying to catch our breath.

"Make me come," she pants before taking my mouth again.

My head is spinning and I'm hard as rock with

nowhere to go. With her words, she nearly made me come.

While she's writhing against me, I'm still conscious of where we are, and who could walk through that door at any moment. But my girl is too far-gone to give a damn.

"Donovan, I'm so close. Please. I ache," she moans.

She's going to kill me.

Shoving my hand between us, I unfasten my jeans and shove them down my thighs, but keep my shorts on—not that they're much of a barrier. Taking a deep breath, I position the root of my dick against her pantie-clad pussy and press down against her before yanking my tee shirt off, letting it drop to the bed.

She fists the duvet and arches up into me with her head thrown back. *Fuckin' gorgeous!*

Pulling the top of her dress down to expose her breasts, I lean down and capture a nipple in my mouth. I slip my hands beneath her. One against her back to keep her arched and one against her bottom—then I start to rock against her and watch as she clamps her mouth shut and starts moving with me.

Moving to her other breast, I massage her nipple with my tongue against the roof of my mouth, and feel her hands slip back into my hair holding me in place, against her.

"Oh God! I'm going to come," she hisses.

She isn't the only one.

I move my hips a fraction to the left and watch as she shakes apart in my arms—gasping and groaning in pleasure. As she starts to get too loud, I release her breast and capture her lips with mine—taking her shouts inside of me. All the while I'm praying for sanity because my balls feel like they're on fire. She surprises the fuck outta me by catching me off guard and flipping me to my back.

As she straddles me, I try to catch my breath, which is impossible with her rocking and grinding against me, while shoving her hands into her hair and throwing her head back. She's a beautiful vision. The girl I've fallen in love with is a sexy nymph. Her breasts are swaying, her nipples begging for my touch.

Releasing her hair, she peels my shorts away from the head of my cock and runs her fingernail between the leaking slit, causing the fire inside me to hover, ready to release. I reach out and roll and pinch her nipples between my fingers. She shoves her chest toward me as she reaches behind her and places her hands on my knees to keep her balance.

I'm going to come.

Rearing up on the bed, I grab Mara and wrapping her up in my arms, I suck her nipple into my mouth. She comes again, sending me with her—white-hot jets spurt out between us, coating my stomach and Mara's dress, between her breasts —everywhere.

Fuck me!

Still quivering with our climax, Mara bites me on the shoulder before pulling slightly away from me with the biggest grin I've ever seen on her face.

"We made a mess."

I close my eyes from the sight of my come between her breasts—her magnificent breasts.

"We need to get cleaned up. You're kind of a mess."

Chuckling, I meet her gaze. "We both are. Thanks to me." I turn her so she's on her back on the bed. "Stay there."

Rolling off the bed, I shove my dick in my shorts and yank my jeans up so I can walk, and quickly make my way to her bathroom. Grabbing the washcloth, I clean my chest before sitting on the john to remove my boots, jeans and shorts. I'll have to go commando until I can get home. Cleaning my cock, I pull my jeans and boots back on. Grabbing a clean cloth, I walk toward the bed unable to help the smug smile that I know is hovering on my face.

"Are you going to clean me up or stand there staring at me all day?"

"I'd love to do both."

Sitting beside her, I run my finger through my cum and rub it around her nipples, which harden under my touch. "I've marked you—much more enjoyable than peeing on your leg."

She bursts out laughing.

Joking aside, it's hot seeing her covered with a part of me, but we've pushed our luck so much right now, that I quickly clean her up before helping her out of her dress.

"Give me a minute to get changed," she says, giving me a quick kiss before slipping from the bed.

Getting up myself, I smooth her bedding out so it doesn't look like we've just taken a tumble in the sack and pull my tee shirt back on. Thank god, I'd taken it off.

Lying back on the bed, staring up at the ceiling, I start to drift off to sleep when I hear the bedroom door open.

As casual as I can, I open my eyes and see the startled look on Sarah's face, but I catch a smile on their mom, Cindy's, face before she hides it from Sarah.

"See. We aren't allowed boys in our rooms, but

Mara has one in hers." She turns and confronts her mom.

"Sarah, stop acting like you're five years old. Donovan isn't a boy."

"Um, excuse me? I was a boy the last time I took a leak," I say to the room at large.

Cindy rolls her eyes. "You're not a boy, you're a man so you're allowed." She winks before turning back to Sarah. "Haven't you still got company on the back porch."

"Humph!" Sarah whirls around and stomps downstairs.

"Is Mara okay? She looked white when she came home."

"Stomach ache," I answer sitting up on the side of the bed. "She's in there getting changed."

"If you need anything just help yourself from downstairs, and Donovan," she waits for my attention to be on her instead of the bathroom door, "I'm trusting you to look after my daughter."

She holds her hand out when I open my mouth to speak but I'm not sure if I'm going to admit that Mara and I are in a relationship or not.

"I know how you feel about her—I'm her mother, I know these things. Just tread carefully with Reece. He's a firecracker waiting to go off. When he does, just remember he'd be the same with anyone going after Mara, and that it isn't personal. You two have a lot of history and it would be heartbreaking to me to see you both fall out for good. I'll do my best to help smooth things between you all if it comes to that because I can't imagine Mara with anyone but you."

"Thank you, and it won't come to that, but Mara's happiness comes first—always."

"Good answer." She closes the door behind her.

"You can come out now."

Mara comes out of the bathroom looking sheepish. I knew she was listening from in there, and in a way, I'm glad she stayed put because I doubt I'd have found out how her mom felt otherwise.

"You look good. Come here, I need you in my arms before I go."

Mara stretches out on top of me, her leg going between mine as she wraps herself around me like a vice.

"I love being in your arms like this. Just the two of us."

"I love that too."

Wrapping her up in my arms and lulling her into sleep, I can't help wondering what Reece is going to have to say once Sarah tells him I've spent time in Mara's room—alone—which she will. Probably.

16

MARA

Donovan left an hour ago not wanting to stay for dinner because he'd overheard Amanda saying that Reece and Callie were going to eat with us this evening. I guess he was right when he said Reece would spend the whole time watching us to see if his suspicions were correct. Because since he took his seat at the dining table with Callie at his side, he's done nothing but throw dark looks in my direction.

My feelings for Donovan are hard to keep at bay at any time, but when he's in the same room as me, I'm probably not going to be able to hide anything.

"So Mara," Reece says, pointing his fork in my direction, "are you going to tell me why my best friend spent the afternoon locked in the bedroom with you."

"Do I have a choice?" I mumble, shoving chicken and carrots into my mouth.

"No you don't."

Sighing, I tell him part truth, "He brought me a book I'd mentioned on the way back home that I'd been looking for. He'd stopped at the store in town looking for something and came across it, so he bought it and drove around here to give it to me. What is wrong with that?" I glare at him, while continuing to eat my dinner.

"There isn't anything wrong with that—the problem I have is him spending all afternoon up there."

"You know what, it really isn't any of your business. Mom knew he was up there with me—discussing my art if you must know—so if Mom's okay with it then I don't see why you can't be."

Stabbing more chicken onto my fork, I practically dare him to say more. He doesn't as Callie is obviously using some distraction technic on him out of the view of the rest of us. *I love Callie.*

The rest of the meal gets finished up pretty quickly in an uncomfortable silence. Reece may have left the discussion alone, but he won't forever. Sarah spent nearly as much time glaring at me as

Reece did. The silence, glares and general unrest isn't because I had a boy up in my room, it's happening because I had Donovan up in my room, which pisses me the hell off.

He might be eight years older than me, my brother's best friend, but I know my own heart. Most of my teenage years have been spent reading and writing about art, most of which is suitable for an adult not a child. My mother has always said I'm more mature than Sarah and Amanda. I'd certainly agree with her about Sarah, and she's just getting worse. Or rather jealousy is rearing it's ugly head.

I'm really not sure how to breach the gap between us or even if we can. There's always been something there, but as I've gotten older, she can't stop with the jabs. Sometimes, I'll look at her after she's made a cutting remark about something I'm doing and she always looks as though she genuinely believes what she's saying.

"Mara, do you have a minute?" Callie asks, gaining a frown from Reece.

"Yeah, sure. What's up?" I ask placing the last of the dishes by the sink for Jessie and Robin to wash and dry.

"Wedding talk."

"Okay. Do you want to go outside for a short walk?"

Callie kisses Reece on the lips and whispers something to him before opening the backdoor and indicating with her hand that I should go first.

I love being outside when it's dusk—not quite day, but not ready to be night yet. It's also a bit cooler, which makes breathing a lot easier because it sure can boil the air in your lungs. Walking with Callie is pleasant. She spends time taking in her surroundings rather than what she has to say. You can bet if I'd been out here with Reece his questions would have started the minute the door had closed. That's one of the things I like about her, not only has she calmed the beast—slightly—but she's good to hang out with.

Walking out along the small dock at the end of our garden, we sit facing the moon with our feet dangling over the water. I lay down, closing my eyes and feel Callie do the same.

After a few minutes of silence, I ask, "Did you really want to talk to me about the wedding?"

"Yes I did, but I could have asked you inside away from your mom. I thought I'd get you out here to find out what is really going on with you and Donovan."

"Start with the wedding, please."

"Okay. I know we've sort of skirted around Dahlia being involved in the wedding, but at the end of the day, she's close to Reece and I'd like her to be included as part of the family and not just a friend. I know Reece wants this, although he hasn't said anything to me."

Once I'd arrived at Donovan's door after the hum dinger of an argument I'd had with Mom over Dahlia, I'd come to realize that Mom wasn't the only one mistreated. Dahlia was left with her bastard of a father—who has finally disappeared and left her alone.

Every time I've seen her since, I've tried to be friendly toward her and I think she's trying as well.

"I really don't know what you're asking me. I'm cool with Dahlia being part of your wedding. I mean it doesn't have anything to do with me anyway, but I'd think it strange if she wasn't involved."

"It's your mom and sisters that Reece is worried about. I am as well. You left because of it all before so we're both hesitant to bring the subject up."

I turn to look at her, and can just make out her eyes in the darkness now the dusk is finally turning to night. "Reece and Mom have made their peace. I talk to Dahlia every time I see her, some of the time I go out of my way to bump in to her. But I know what you're saying. You don't want your big day ruined because my mom or one of my sisters says something upsetting to her, right?"

"Yeah."

"Look, don't worry about it. I'll mention it to Mom when I go back inside and hopefully she won't lose it again."

She grins in the dark showing me her white teeth. "Now. I want to know exactly what is going on between Donovan and you—not the Reece version—the Callie version."

Groaning, I close my eyes again and think about my guy holding me all afternoon as we both slept. I know we got up to no good before that, but he just held me even though there was a chance of someone else barging into my room.

"That good, huh?"

I giggle. "Oh yeah!" I curl up on my side and resting my head in my hand, I admit, "He makes me happy, Callie. Really, really happy. I've wanted him to notice me for so long. Now that he does, I keep having to pinch myself to make sure it's real and I'm not dreaming." I lay back down. "Although I've wanted him for a while I'm glad it's taken this long for us to get together because I feel ready to be with him. I don't just mean sex, I mean to be with him—to spend time with him and just hang out. But he's worried about Reece, and I guess I am as well. You know what Reece is like with me Callie. I just don't get why he'd be against me being with his best friend."

"I don't think you want to go there Mara."

"I know what Reece and Donovan used to get up to before Reece fell for you so I guess I can understand that. But Reece has proved he can settle on one girl and be happy so why can't Donovan. I mean sometimes Reece looks so damn in love with you that it makes me want to hurl."

"Ha ha ha. You're funny—not."

I nudge her. "Yes it was—you've made my brother a love sick idiot."

"Yeah, well, he's my idiot and I love him and can't wait to get his ring on my finger. What are you going to do about Donovan and telling Reece?"

"I really don't know. Jack suggested after the wedding—"

"Wait. Jack knows?"

"Um, yeah. He kind of caught us this morning on Donovan's kitchen floor."

"But, I mean. Shit. You've done it with him?"

"I wish I could say yes, but we've only fooled around. He didn't have any condoms, otherwise, I'm sure we would have done. And now I'm on my period so that takes care of the next few days."

I can practically feel the wheels turning in Callie's head as we continue to lay side-by-side. It would be nice if I could talk to one of my sisters like I can with Callie. Jessie and Robin are too young for this kind of discussion, but Sarah and Amanda aren't. I won't talk to Sarah because I don't get along with her, and I'd be putting Amanda on the spot with Sarah if I told her too much. Not with the intention of hurting me, but because she thinks we're sisters and that we all can be trusted.

"Thinking about Reece, all I know is that you both need to tell him before he finds out because that will just make things twice as bad. It's also going to kill me knowing this and he doesn't."

"I know. By telling you I've put you in an awkward position. I'm really sorry. I shouldn't have said anything."

"No. Don't say that. I'm glad that you feel comfortable talking to me knowing I'm your brother's girl. In fact, it makes me feel really good."

I smile, although Callie probably can't see now that it's pitch black outside.

"Thank you for driving my brother crazy and making him chase you. That's what he needed to be brought down a peg or two by a girl. I love him, but he's an idiot some times."

"Whose an idiot?" Reece says causing us both to jump into a sitting position in surprise.

"What are you doing out here? You promised to give us some privacy."

Reece switches the lights on along the small dock before he comes over to us.

"I think I've given you enough private time with my little sister. Now it's future husband time." Reece sits behind Callie and pulls her into his chest before nuzzling her neck.

Turning my head away to gaze out across the water, toward the lights on the opposite side, I can't help but wish that Donovan was here with me. I wish that I was snuggling in his arms, feeling safe from the world.

My heart is telling me to shout that he's my guy and that I'm in love with him. But my brain it telling me to wait—that now isn't the right time. The thing is though, I'm not sure there will ever be a right time to announce my relationship with Donovan. Reece will flip out regardless, and a huge part of me wants to get it over with. But for the wedding, I probably would have blurted it out, but it would break my heart if I ruined my brother and Callie's wedding.

I swipe at a tear feeling sorry for myself—feeling alone. Donovan would be here with me if I asked him to be. That I know without a doubt. He'd be cautious, but he'd be here.

"Mara, are you okay?" Reece asks, concern for me clear in his voice.

Getting to my feet, I whisper, "I will be," before turning and heading back toward the house, needing some space from the loving couple.

I also need to hear Donovan's voice, if only for a minute. So running up to my room, I lock my bedroom door and disconnecting the charger, I flop down on to my bed. Laying on my stomach to quickly shoot Donovan a text. I unlock the phone and discover to my delight that I have three text messages from him.

Missing you

Missing you even more

I grin—he's an idiot, who's making my heart beat rapidly in my chest.

I'm sitting out back, drinking a longneck wondering what you're doing, whom you're talking to and most of all, I'm wishing that I was with you <3

As tears run down my face, I swipe at them so I can see the keys to reply to him.

You have no idea how much I wish you had been with me. I watched Callie and Reece snuggling together and wanted that to have been us. <3

Then I add,

I miss you <3

Within seconds a text arrives back from him.

Soon baby. That will be us real soon. Just a few more days <3 sweet dreams <3

Is he getting rid of me?

You don't want to talk?

I do but I can't keep my eyes open. Tiredness and alcohol don't mix well.

After about a minute while I debate with myself whether or not I can get away with sneaking to his place, I send him a text back.

Okay. I'll see you tomorrow. Dream of me <3

I always dream of you <3

Sighing, I don't bother to remove my clothes and slip beneath the quilt. I'm really tired as well.

17

DONOVAN

It's been three days since I saw Mara and I'm beginning to get frustrated as hell. The day following our loving in her bedroom, she'd woken with a migraine and had stayed in bed all day. My first instinct was to go straight around there to see her for myself, but I'd spoken to Cindy and she'd assured me that Mara would be all right and was being looked after. Reece had been there so she didn't think it was wise for me to come round. No matter how much it hurt, I stayed away.

And now I'm about to see her with all her family at the rehearsal dinner, which is being held at the country club. In an earlier text, Mara told me she was dressing for me tonight. My only hope is that Reece doesn't notice the reaction my body has because of her. I mean the last thing he needs is to catch me with a physical hard-on for his sister that would really go down well.

Pulling into the lot, I spot Mia and Liam walking into the place. The country club isn't one of my favorite places, but I can see why Jack's parents would have arranged to have the rehearsal dinner here. It's like any other country club—full of pretentious snobs.

With a bit of luck, Reece will be distracted with Callie's family having arrived in town earlier today.

Stepping out of my truck, I'm just about to head toward the entrance when I catch movement from the corner of my eye. I turn and watch Dahlia marching off in front of Ryder as though they've had an argument. I didn't even know they were dating, but perhaps they won't be for long.

On entering the foyer with it's grand crystal chandelier, dark wood, mahogany walls, and centuries old oil paintings on the walls, all I can think about is escaping the place with my girl. This isn't part of my world and I don't feel as though I belong here. It isn't because of money—I have plenty of that, thanks to my parents' savings and insurance policy, but this whole place makes me itch. Some of the folks who hang out here are okay and tell it as they see it, but others are so full of shit.

"I hate this place." Jack pulls me back into the here and now. "Thalia isn't all that keen either, but went along with it because of what my folks wanted. I'm sure as hell glad that we put our feet down about the wedding."

"I know what you mean. Every time I walk through that door I expect to see Dorkins with his top hat on greeting everyone. Do you remember him from when we were kids?"

Jack laughs. "He's one of the only happy memories I have of this place. Everyone else used to look at us like we were dirt on the floor when our dads would bring us here, but not him."

"No, he didn't. He used to frighten the shit outta us at first though."

"Speak for yourself. He never frightened me," Jack adds.

I grin, raising an eyebrow as Jack slaps me on the back and disappears to claim his soon to be bride.

Huh, not him—yeah, right!

Surveying the room for Mara, I don't see her anywhere until I'm on my second pass through and see her smiling at me from across the room.

My feet have suddenly turned to lead as I take her in. She is the most beautiful girl here. Her curves are covered in the dark wine dress she'd been having fitted at the dress store, the skirt dropping to her high-heeled covered feet. As she moves toward me, my dick thickens and lengthens. There is a slit in the dress right up to nearly the top of her thigh, which I missed in the dress store—one inch higher and she'd be showing her pussy when she moved.

As she gets closer to me, I notice her nipples poking through the dress, and all I want to do is take my jacket off and wrap her up in it so no one else gets to see her like that—*sexy*.

She comes to a stop directly in front of me, and briefly presses against me, sending a surge of lust so strong through my body, she's lucky I don't grab her over my shoulder and run off to have my way with her.

"You're beautiful and killing me."

"I know. You look handsome in your suit. All the girls are going to be drooling over you."

"How do you think I'm going to feel knowing the guys are going to be imagining you naked?"

"They can imagine all they want because you're the only one who is going to get to see me naked—tonight." She steps closer so her nipples are rubbing against my jacket and my cock is pressing into her hip. "I no longer have the female problem," she whispers, "so you can touch, stroke, lick, and penetrate me there to your heart's content." My dick surges against her. She grins up at me.

"You are playing with fire, babe," I growl.

"I'm soon going to be playing with you." She turns and walks into the private room where tonight's dinner is taking place leaving me with my tongue stuck to the roof of my mouth.

I've always found her sexy, but I've never seen her as the sexy siren before.

"The great Donovan has fallen," Jack chuckles, "but I'd close your jacket and get that sappy look off your face before Reece catches you.

"Did you see her?" I mumble, running my hands through my hair in an effort to loosen my lust-ridden body up. "I mean, *fuck*."

"C'mon. Get your brain from what's beneath that dress and let's go and take our seats so we can change the seating if we don't like whose next to us." Jack gives me a shove, which gets my feet moving.

"I hate to break this to you, but you're not going to get that privilege on this occasion as it's your rehearsal dinner. My guess is you'll be sitting between Thalia and her mom." I grin. That shut him up.

But my grin slips as I see my sexy siren in the seat next to where I've just been directed making sweet talk to the guy beside her. *I don't think so.*

Quickly stalking over to the table, I yank my chair out and drop into it much to Mara's amusement. The guy on her left frowns over at me. Probably realizing his chances with this delicious babe have just gone out through the window.

"Donovan, this is Matt. A cousin of Thalia's."

"Hi Matt," I lean forward and shake his hand, "nice to meet you." I'm tempted to make a claim on my girl in front of the guy, but then I can't guarantee he isn't going to open his mouth in Reece's hearing.

Sitting back in my seat, I ignore him. In fact, I end up ignoring everyone for the next ten minutes. My head suddenly feels like it's going to explode with the stress of hiding from my friends. It feels like I'm ashamed of being with Mara, which is so far from the truth. I've never been good at lying, which is probably why the guys always used to make sure my mouth was full with food whenever we were being questioned about something we'd gotten up to.

"What's wrong," Mara asks as I feel her hand on my thigh waking my shaft up.

"I hate sitting beside you and not being able to touch you. You're mine Mara. I hate not being up front with everyone," I whisper under my breath.

"I hate that too." Her hand creeps further north and now rests inches from where I ache for her touch.

"Keep going," I hiss.

It's killing me not pressing up into her hand, but right now I'm thanking my lucky stars that the tablecloth is long and pools in my lap.

Her hand lands on my balls as she presses down, she moves along my growing length—then *fuck*— she has my zipper down and is reaching in for my erection. This is so not a good idea. I try to move out of her grasp, but she holds tight and finally frees me.

I gulp and my legs quiver with her finger rubbing against the slit on the head of my dick. The more she caresses me, the harder I'm getting, which is a shocker as I already thought I was hard as fuck.

"I want to taste you," she breathes into my neck.

My dick surges in her hand. I'm going to be so fuckin' lucky if I don't come with her hand on me beneath the table.

148

"Oops. I dropped my knife," Mara says before ducking under the tablecloth.

Then for mere seconds I feel her mouth sucking on the head of my cock before she's sitting back in her seat again with a devilish grin on her face. Turning to me, she licks her lips and shoves me back into my trousers and fastens them. I suppose I should be glad she didn't get me with the zipper.

Closing my eyes, I try to catch my breath and when I open them I see Sarah across the table glaring at us. I grin and then proceed to take notice of my surroundings to try and get the lust for the girl beside me out of my body.

Okay Donovan, concentrate on the room.

The room that used to give me the creeps about twenty years ago when I'd sneak in to get out of the way of the adults. I think it had more to do with the darkness of the room because back then it was dark and gloomy and had the look of Frankenstein's house. I always blamed Reece for that as it was him who'd snuck the movie out of the house so we all could watch it on the VCR his dad had set up for us in part of the double garage. I don't think I slept for a month after that.

Well at least the décor has been modernized, in fact it doesn't look that bad now from what I can see with the dimmed lighting. The room isn't large, but elegant and they seem to have a thing about chandeliers.

"Prawns," the server asks, jerking my attention to him. Before I can answer a fancy glass is placed in front of me with the horrid stuff inside. I hate prawns.

Mara chuckles beside me, and pushes her glass slightly away from her place setting.

"Eat up," she says, knowing good and well that I hate the suckers.

"Why don't you eat up?" I grin, knowing good and well that she hates them too.

She pulls a face. "No chance."

I push mine away because there is no way I can be polite and eat them. I can stomach some things that I'm not all that keen on, but prawns aren't one of them.

Leaning close to Mara's ear, I whisper, "You could suck the sauce off like you used to do as a kid."

She turns to face me, and whispers back, "I'd rather be sucking on something else." Her breath caresses my lips in the process.

And that's all it takes to get my blood rushing straight to my groin. As I lengthen in anticipation of having her mouth on me again for longer than a few seconds, my eyes narrow.

She has the upper hand right now, but remembering the slit in her skirt she isn't going to have it for much longer.

Slipping my hand under the cloth, I place my palm on her thigh and smile when I hear the breath catch in her throat in a kind of gurgling, choking noise.

"Are you all right, Mara?" Matt asks.

"Yes. Fine. Just a bit warm."

Taking a handful of her dress, I tune out her conversation with him and sigh when my hand finally comes into contact with flesh. I slowly move my hand closer and closer to the heat I know will be waiting for me and when I finally make contact she hisses through her teeth as I pause.

She isn't wearing any fuckin' panties. *Fuck me!* As I slide my finger down between the lips of her pussy, she opens her legs for me and I feel how wet she is, nearly coming on the spot. Coating my fingers in her essence, I dip inside her and feel the walls of her sex quivering around my fingers as I add another one.

My dick is trying to punch through my slacks and as I glance down to Mara's breasts her nipples are rock hard buds against the silk material of her dress. I need to taste her. I need to be on my knees between her legs with my mouth buried in her pussy.

Suddenly pushing my hand away, she gets to her feet, and whispers, "Follow me. NOW."

My brows nearly reach my hairline. How the fuck does she expect me to walk? But the promise of her naked flesh makes me think to hell with this so as soon as the lights dip again, I quickly make my way toward the restrooms.

18

MARA

THE RESTROOMS HERE ARE MORE LIKE HOTEL suites and are laid out individually, which is so to my advantage right now. My only excuse for my behavior is Donovan. He's awakened something inside me, not something, I know exactly what it is—he's awakened my sexual appetite. I'm an eighteen-year-old virgin and can't keep my hands off my *boyfriend*. I love teasing him and watching him react to my closeness or even just my smile directed at him.

When I chose the dress I'm wearing tonight, I'd chosen it with him in mind. At the time I had no plans to seduce him though—those plans just appeared in my head the minute I'd seen the lust clear on his face. My dress doesn't allow for underwear so that had been an added bonus.

Hearing footsteps outside, I crack the door open slightly and see Donovan appear in my line of sight. As he gets closer, I reach out and pull him into the room. He slams the door shut and shoves the lock into place. We're alone.

I move to rest against the vanity, facing him. My eyes travel back and forth over him, but keep getting pulled back to his hips where there is an impressive bulge behind his zipper.

"You are driving me insane," he growls, cupping his length through the material of his slacks.

I gulp watching him touch himself. The throb between my legs is growing to unbearable proportions.

Without moving my eyes from his, I reach under my arm for the zipper to my dress and slowly pull it down, catching the material as it moves away from my breasts. When the zipper stops, I lift the material from around my neck and then let the dress pool at my feet before bending down to pick it up to lay it over the chair. After all, I'll have to put it back on afterwards.

Donovan is speechless in front of me as he takes in my nakedness with *fuck-me* shoes still on my feet. I'm not oblivious to his reaction and feel a desperation to have his twitching dick in my hands. I didn't think he could get any bigger but he lengthens and widens before my eyes. It's a wonder his zipper hasn't burst.

Taking two steps forward, I drop to my knees and make quick work of opening his slacks only to hear him hiss between his teeth as I circle his girth with one hand and reach to massage his sac with the other. His slacks drop around his ankles while he tosses his jacket, tie and shirt onto the chair with my dress.

His hands massage my shoulders as he goes tense when I lick him from root to the leaking head of his dick—more pre-cum leaking out the more I lick him.

While I'm pleasuring him, I'm aching badly for him to touch me, which he can't do if I'm on my knees at his feet. I let him fall from my mouth after one powerful suck, and hold my hand out for him to help me up, which he does.

Standing close to him, I massage him down to his balls before pushing him between my legs. He's so long that I can feel him rubbing against my backside as well.

He drops his forehead against mine and grips my hips in a tight hold as his breathing accelerates.

"I need to be inside you."

"I need you inside me."

"I can't, your first time isn't going to be in the

restroom of the country club. It's going to be in a bed with candles lit around the room and soft music in the background."

He's killing me.

"Please do something. I need relief that only you can give me. You need it as well."

As though a switch has been turned, he lifts me, struggles to the vanity with his slacks around his ankles and turns me around. He places both my hands on the vanity in front of me and spreads my legs, pulling my hips out toward him.

Quickly kicking off his shoes and getting himself free of his shorts and slacks, his hands are back on me.

"You've had me hard as fuck all evening," he says slowly caressing from my shoulder down past my bottom before he strokes between my folds and groans. "So wet." He then caresses back up to my neck.

He arches into me and shoves his balls between my legs with his dick between the crease of my bottom. Just that bit of friction has my inner walls clenching, trying to get him inside me. Pressing his front against my back, he whispers in to my ear, "You're going to come on my balls and fingers. I'm going to come all over you—we're getting dirty babe." His hands reach around to the front of me as he starts to pinch my nipples.

Pleasure shoots from them straight to my throbbing center as I grind back against him wanting more—so much more.

"Donovan. Please."

One hand strokes my pussy as he inserts two fingers inside me. I clench around them and feel heat spread throughout my body. He's surrounding me and it feels like he's touching me everywhere at once on my breasts, in my sex, rubbing against my bottom. It's too much. The coil inside me twists to a hard knot and then with a quick thrust of his fingers, it starts to unwind so quickly I can't keep up with it. My breath sticks in my throat. Then I see stars. My pussy ripples with the tremors of my climax as I clamp my teeth together to stop from alerting everyone to the fact that I'm having an orgasm.

Donovan isn't letting up. I pull his hand away from me, unable to take anymore.

"Fuck," Donovan cusses pulling slightly away from me.

Still bent over the vanity, I turn my head and watch him take his dick into his hand and pumping his shaft once, twice, he comes all over my bottom. Massaging it into me with the tip of his cock.

He finally meets my eyes and I see a blush start to coat his cheekbones.

"Are you all right?"

I nod.

He grabs some napkins and after running them underneath the faucet, wipes me clean—not just my back but between my legs before patting me dry.

"Let's get dressed." He passes me my dress.

Not looking at me—ignoring me—he dresses so I follow suit wondering what the hell has just happened.

Once my dress is on and fastened back up, I quickly sort my hair out and reapply some lipstick before taking a deep breath to face Donovan and whatever is going on in his head.

"I'm sorry."

Fighting back tears, I ask, "Sorry for what? I need it explained to me so there isn't any misunderstanding."

He runs his hands through his hair. "I'm sorry for the kinky, dirty sex or whichever way you want to look at it."

Now I'm confused.

"I've no idea what you're talking about. I loved every minute of being in here with you."

"Coming on you. Marking you. It isn't right." He blushes again.

It's kind of sweet and I sag in relief that's he's embarrassed about covering me with his cum rather than getting naked with me.

"I'm yours Donovan whether you like it or not. Coming on and marking me with your scent is *fuckin'* hot, and if you apologize for ever doing that I'm going to hurt you—badly. Do I make my self clear?"

He grins. "Yes ma'am."

Ugh!

"And one more thing—don't ever call me ma'am. I know you're a southern boy, but I'm eighteen not seventy."

He cups my face in his hands. "I know exactly how old you are." He kisses me. "You are the most beautiful woman I've ever seen." He kisses me again. "Please try to keep your hands to yourself for the rest of the evening."

"I will," I cheekily reply while smacking him on the butt.

He growls.

"How are we going to explain our disappearance?"

That is something I never gave thought to.

"I ate a prawn and got sick." I shrug. "You know how much I hate prawns, well so do my family so it's realistic."

"If you hate them why would you try and eat one?"

"Okay then. How about I couldn't see what I was eating and as soon as it was in my mouth I wanted to hurl and came running to the restrooms and you followed to make sure I was all right."

He shakes his head. "You realize how stupid that sounds, right?"

"Yeah, but if we both say the same thing and *mean it* then I don't see the problem."

I smile. "C'mon."

Donovan groans as I open the door. I know my excuse is lame, but as I left the private room first it makes sense that I could have been sick and Donovan was worried about me. If I had to guess though I'd say no matter what I just told him, he still feels embarrassed at coming all over my bottom. I didn't lie when I told him it was hot. I love the fact that I make him lose it like that. I've read books with dirtier things in them than what we've just done. I find that hot.

About to open the door into the private room, Donovan snakes his arm around my stomach.

"You go in first. I'm going to get some fresh air outside. It might not look as bad if we go in separately."

"Okay," I agree.

He kisses me on the back of my neck, sending shivers down my spine and making my nipples harden for his attention. Before I can fully turn, he's released me. I turn and watch him stride past the stairs and out of the main doors to the club.

"Mara."

I freeze hearing my name on Sarah's lips.

19

DONOVAN

I'M COMING UNHINGED. THE IDEA OF GOING back into that room and being unable to touch my girl is about to tear me in two. I love her, and that thought makes me want to hurl. I've never let anyone in to my heart before, but she's been in it for a while now, and the more time I spend with her the harder it is to keep us a secret.

She's eight years younger than me, although to be more exact, she is a little over seven years younger by about five months. But the thought of her age is giving me a headache. I'm not going to walk away from her though—I can't. God, I wish I smoked right about now.

After what we've just done in there I should be stress free, but no such luck.

"So this is where you disappeared to," Reece drawls coming to stand beside me.

"Yeah. Aren't you needed in there?" I point with my head in the direction we've both just come from.

"I need some fresh air." He rubs his finger between his neck and collar. "I don't know why I have to wear this thing when the wedding isn't until tomorrow."

I grin. "Callie really does have you in a noose."

"You have no idea. That girl has me wearing a hard-on for her 24/7. I'm surprised it's not snapped in two by now."

I wince. "Did I really need to know that?"

He laughs. "I guess not."

He eyes me from the corner of his eye and I know he's appraising me. "I thought you disappeared off somewhere with Mara, but I guess I'm wrong. Am I wrong?"

Fuck!

"Partly." I hate this. "She suddenly disappeared from the room with her hand over her mouth so I followed to check on her. She was sick. Apparently she ate one of the prawns not realizing what they were because of the dimmed lighting." I shrug my shoulders. "She seemed okay when she went back in to the room, but I needed some fresh air."

I'm staring out toward the golf course and can feel his eyes on me, trying to gauge whether or not I'm telling him the truth. I can honestly say that until Mara, I haven't lied to him. Not once. And now I feel like the biggest dick around.

"You coming back inside?" he asks, obviously reading truth in my statement. I really feel sick.

"Rehearsal starting yet?"

"In thirty."

"I'll be back in for that."

"Okay." He walks back inside and leaves me with my screwed up thoughts again.

Turning to gaze up at the stars, Dahlia bursts through the doors causing a ruckus followed closely by Ryder who looks pissed. I lean back against the porch railings and watch.

"You are an insensitive jerk," Dahlia shouts over her shoulder at him.

His jaw hardens as he grabs her arm and turns her to look at him. "What the fuck Dahlia? They are your half sisters and you're letting them walk all over you and treat you like shit. Don't take your temper out on me."

"Not all of them are," she whispers sounding upset and Ryder seems to deflate at her words.

He takes her hand. "C'mon. I'm taking you

home. I'm not letting you be subjected to them again tonight."

I watch as they disappear to Ryder's truck.

Ryder and Dahlia. Who knew they'd get together, and who's against Dahlia? The top of my list for causing trouble would have to be Sarah. I can't imagine Mara being in the middle of anything at least not where Dahlia is concerned considering she always goes out of her way to talk to her.

"Hey," Mara interrupts, slipping her hand into mine.

Wrapping my fingers around hers, I bring her hand up to my lips for a quick kiss.

"Hey, yourself. Won't you be missed?"

"Not yet. Reece asked me to come get you."

I frown at her words. "He did?"

"Yeah. I'm not sure what he's up to, but I'm not going to complain because I need to touch you."

I look more closely at her and she looks nervous. Pulling my hand free, I cup her face and pull her gently into me. "Tell me."

Her eyes close before she opens them but with tears on her lashes. Leaning down, I kiss each one before resting my forehead against hers—one of my favorite places—wondering what the hell has happened.

"Sarah saw us together." My eyes widen as she

offers me a wry smile. "She caught sight of us leaving the restroom and waited until you'd disappeared before letting me know."

Realizing she's worried and needs comfort, I pull her into my arms and hold her close. Right now while I'm trying to reassure her with my arms around her, I don't care who the hell sees us. She's my girl and this is my right.

Tell that to Reece!

"What did she say?"

"Just that she knows you're making me sneak around with you and that I need to stop before she tells Reece."

"I told her that we'd be telling Reece and no one else would be. She didn't like that and called me a few choice words before I stomped on her foot and went back into the room." She kisses me on the neck before settling back against my chest. "The thing is I really don't know why she's being like she is. She's my sister. Sisters are suppose to stand together not be a *bitch*."

Unable to keep the laughter bubbling inside me at bay, I let it out much to Mara's disgust. "Sorry, babe." I chuckle. "I know it isn't funny—this situation with Sarah," I explain, "but you calling her a bitch, tickled me."

She rolls her eyes. "We better go and join the others so we don't screw up tomorrow."

"In a minute. I want to hold you in my arms a bit longer before I have to act as though you don't belong with me." I kiss the top of her head. "It kills me seeing Jack and Reece happily wrapped around their girls when I can't even hold your hand in front of them," I admit. The next thing I hear is her sniffling against me. *Is she crying?*

"Mara?"

She shakes her head but stays buried in my chest.

"Mara, babe. I'm sorry. I didn't mean to make you cry."

I finally get her to lift her head and it crushes me when I see the tears on her face.

"It hurts me as well," she whispers, "and now I'm not even sure I can go out there and pretend my feelings for you are platonic."

More tears escape her eyes and run toward my waiting thumbs, but I can't bear this anymore so I lean in and start using my lips to catch them all before placing a tender kiss to each corner of her mouth.

"Hold me. Hold me tight and never let me go."

Pulling her back in to my arms, I do what she asks, although I am going to have to let her go. But for now I can comfort my girl, and in the process comfort me.

"Everyone is looking for you two," Jack says from behind me.

Mara tightens her grip around my waist.

"Give us a minute."

"That's all you've got. If I hadn't overheard Reece telling Callie he was coming looking for you, he'd be the one standing here, although I don't think much standing would be taking place."

He's right.

"I hear you." I kiss Mara on the forehead and gaze into her eyes. "Will you be okay?"

She nods and tries to offer me a smile, but it ends up being more like a wince than anything else.

"We can do this. Only a couple more days."

"I guess." Stepping out of my arms, she walks over to Jack and gives him a surprise hug, whispering, "Thank you," into his ear.

"I'm just going to clean up so I'll meet you there," Mara says heading back inside.

She looks a lot better now than she did earlier, which is a relief. I just hope she holds it together long enough to get through tonight's rehearsal before the big day tomorrow afternoon.

Jack stands beside me but stays silent—lost in his own thoughts. Then after about five minutes, he says, "No matter what you've told me before about how she makes you feel, I found it hard to believe because of her age, but seeing you together like this and how much it was hurting you to see her in tears, I truly believe you're in love with her," Jack finishes on a smug grin.

"I'm not going to deny it because it's true."

"What's true?" Mara asks obviously catching the tail end of my statement.

"Me and you." I slide my hand into hers. "C'-mon, lets go before they send out another search party."

20

MARA

"Mara, can you go and find Dahlia? Reece is freaking out because she isn't answering her cell and you're the only one who goes out of your way to talk to her."

Rolling my eyes, I open my bedroom door to my mom who has been shouting through it about Dahlia. I do get along with her whenever we bump into each other although she was difficult to talk to at the beginning. I don't blame her really, but I'm happy my mom seems to have accepted her in this whole *weird* situation.

"Please Mara. You know Reece isn't going to settle until she's accounted for."

"I'll go," I drop to my bed, "but I only have—"

"Two hours," Mom finishes for me.

"Fran is already here to start on everyone's hairstyles and she's in Jessie and Robin's room so you and Dahlia can be last. Just go now." Mom starts picking my shoes up from my floor before throwing them into my closet. "Make sure you call Reece as soon as you find her so he can calm down and concentrate on giving me another daughter and maybe a grandchild."

My eyes widen and I start laughing. "I think for now they're enjoying the *practice* of baby making more than actually *making* one."

"Your brother is very protective of those he loves. He needs a huge distraction to take his mind off what you and Donovan are doing."

"Um."

Doing?

"Mom."

"Oh, for goodness sake Mara. You're eighteen years old—a woman. I don't expect you to discuss *things* with me, but I'm not blind." She stands in front of me, pushing the loose strands of my hair from my forehead. "You bloom, baby. Whenever he walks into the house, your whole face lights up," she smiles, "and when you're not looking he can't take his eyes from you. I know, I more or less, gave you my blessing before, but honey, as soon as Reece is married you need to tell him that you're in love with his best friend. It isn't fair to Donovan and you, and it isn't fair to Reece. He loves you both." She kisses me on my cheek. "Now I've spoken my wonderful words of wisdom go and find your half-sister."

She leaves me surprised in my bedroom. "Half-sister?"

I'm happy that she's being cool about Dahlia today. God knows Dahlia could do with some friends in this house.

Slipping my feet into my boots, I grab my cell and manage to escape the wedding madness here.

It's crazy, but I love it, and I can't wait to witness my brother marrying Callie this afternoon, something that I certainly didn't think would happen anytime soon. My mind of course jumps to my guy, Donovan. Wondering what he's up to. Wondering if he's ready to deck Reece from stressing out over Dahlia. I know I would be, I'm not the most patient of people.

Deciding that I need to talk to him, I press short cut three on my cell and listen as it starts to ring on his end.

"Morning babe," he answers.

"Morning."

"Mara, what's wrong?"

"Does something have to be wrong for me to call you?"

"No, but you sound odd—out of sorts."

"I'm good, but I'm on my way to Kix, hoping Dahlia is going to be there. Apparently Reece can't get hold of her so I figured I'd start there with her being with Ryder last night."

"Where are you now?"

"At the crossroads," I reply waving to Mr. Frederickson driving his 1953 Cadillac into town. It's a gorgeous car, one that he's obviously spent a fortune on keeping in good condition. It's a pity it doesn't go much faster, although I have a feeling that has more to do with the driver than the vehicle.

"I'll meet you at Kix. You shouldn't be going there on your own."

I laugh. "Donovan, it's mid-morning not midnight."

"You're not twenty-one yet. I'm not sure Ryder will let you in."

Why didn't I think of that? In fact, why didn't my mother think of that?

"I'll wait outside."

"Okay, babe. I'll be there in five. Bye."

"Bye."

Now that I'm going to be seeing Donovan, my step feels lighter. I'd wanted to go home with him last night after the rehearsal, but he wouldn't let me. He said he wanted me too much to not make love to me, and that he hadn't had time to get the things he wanted to make my first time special.

I wasn't too impressed at first but his sweet kisses along with his sweet talk had worked magic on me. So I'd gone home with my family to have a very frustrating night's sleep.

I'm still tired, but the excitement of the day will carry me along, and now as I'm approaching Kix I can't help feel apprehensive at what's going on with Dahlia. She's having a hard time coming to terms with everything now that it's out in the open and I guess my sisters aren't really helping. Jessie and Robin are blaming her for Dad being such a dick, Amanda has been pleasant, but of course Sarah's been the bitch that she's become. I guess it can't be easy for Dahlia not really having anyone to fall back on because Reece is in the middle of the whole thing, but he's been distracted with Callie for a while now.

Before I can drop to the steps, Donovan comes racing into the lot out front of Kix leaving dust in his wake. He pulls to a stop in front of me, and jumping out of his truck strides toward me with purpose. Ripping his shades off, he grabs me by the bottom, pulling me into him. My arms go around his neck as his mouth descends on mine.

Our tongues tangle, my pussy quivers. God, it

has taken seconds for me to go from zero to ten. I wrap my legs around his waist and grind against the hardness I feel in my most sensitive place. I can't get enough of him as I chase his tongue back into his mouth, our moans mingle the higher our passion rises. His hands on my bottom squeeze and start to help me grind against him, but he pulls his mouth free and stills my movement.

"Wow," he gulps. "That was unexpected," he tells me in a rough voice sounding sexy as hell.

"I missed you." I rotate my hips and I'm delighted when he gasps and puts me away from him.

"We shouldn't be doing this out here." He breathes out while leaning against his truck. The distance between us is only a few feet, but I need to be close to him so I step closer and watch as his eyes darken. "I'm trying to get my body under control and you're not helping."

"My body is just as out of control as yours is, but I need you close," I whisper, resting against him with my arms going around his waist as I inhale his woodsy scent into my lungs.

"Don't we have a girl to find?"

Dahlia. I'd forgotten.

"We do."

"Before we do though I think I need to tell you what I overheard last night. When her and Ryder were leaving the club, she told him someone in your family was pretty bad to her. At least that's how I took what she was saying to him."

"That doesn't surprise me. I'd bet it was Sarah, although it could have been Jessie or Robin. Amanda's pretty cool with her and so is my mom, now."

"C'mon." He takes my hand and pulls me up the steps. "Let's go and find her because, if I have to guess, Reece is driving everyone crazy wanting to find her."

"I'm surprised he's not here himself."

"I spoke to him on the way here to see if he'd heard from her and he said Callie will kill him if he goes AWOL on their wedding day."

"That figures," I mumble.

Donovan opens the door.

"I hope she's here," I say looking around the place.

Walking inside Kix for the first time, I'm surprised at how clean and nice it is. There are wooden tables throughout the place that look to have a shine to them as though they are new and the walls are covered with all kinds of memorabilia. Everything looks to have a home, which makes the place neat and tidy, but welcoming as well.

"Hey Ryder." Donovan drags my gaze to the guy who is responsible for the transformation, which has happened here. The whole town was a buzz with gossip during the renovation.

If he's surprised at seeing us together it doesn't show as he walks closer and shakes Donovan's hand before reaching for mine.

"What brings you two in here? Don't you have a wedding to be at?"

"That's what brings us here. We're looking for Dahlia. Reece is going crazy not being able to get hold of her."

His eyes darken. "I know you've been good to her Mara, but other members of your family have done nothing but make her life a nightmare. She just wants to be left alone."

"I know what my family is like, I put up with enough shit as it is from one of my sisters, but I really like Dahlia and Reece is going to go crazy if she isn't at his wedding. Please Ryder. Do you know where she is?"

He assesses us for a few minutes before pointing toward the back with his head. "She's back there. Don't upset her."

"We won't," I reassure him wondering what's going on between them both.

Donovan gives a tug on my hand, which gets me moving with him to the door at the side of the bar.

Pulling me through, he closes it behind me and pushes me up against it.

"You looked him over."

I laugh.

He doesn't.

"You're serious?"

He glares at me.

I roll my eyes, and feel a bout of teasing come over me.

"He's a hot guy," I reply.

He growls.

I slip my hand beneath his tee shirt and drag my nails over his stomach and smile when I feel it quiver.

"You're not distracting me."

Oh, yes I am.

Dipping my finger into the front of his jeans, he hisses and closes his eyes as I feel the tip of his aroused flesh. I rub along the leaking slit.

"You're going to have me coming in my jeans."

Pulling my finger out, I slowly slide it into my mouth. While he watches, I let him see my tongue curl around my finger and then I suck it before letting it plop out of my mouth.

"That. Was. Cruel."

"Let's go and find Dahlia." I take his hand this time and grin as he adjusts the bulge in his jeans.

Thank god I've read a lot of books and know just how to tease a hot-blooded male. It gives me a thrill knowing that I can reduce him to a throbbing hard-on with words and a touch.

Outside, I spot Dahlia sitting on a log at the end of the forest, which borders the back of Kix. Her head is lowered with her face in her hands.

Rubbing my temples, I turn to Donovan, and ask, "Would you mind waiting here for me? She might be more comfortable with me—female to female."

"I'll wait here." He gives me a quick kiss before dropping on his ass to the back steps.

Dahlia watches me as I walk toward her. Her expression is neutral, but as my gaze stays focused on her, I see it starting to slip. I can't help wishing my brother had told us all about her way back when he had discovered her secret. Perhaps if he had, we could have grown up being friends as well. I like her. I always have although on one or two occasions, I've been jealous because of the relationship she has with Reece. I also feel sorry for her as well because she hasn't had it good. The man who raised her as his daughter is a bastard and has mistreated her for years. I don't mean physically, at least I don't think that happened, but there are a lot of other ways to mistreat someone. I'm just glad he's disappeared.

Sitting beside her on the log, I look up and see Donovan sitting outside Kix where he said he'd wait for me. He's still there and looks damn cute.

"You and Donovan?" Dahlia asks.

"Yeah," then I turn to face her, "but please don't tell Reece. We're going to tell him after his wedding. In a day or two. He's going to hit the roof so I'd rather not ruin his wedding."

"He loves you and only wants what's best. He's spent too much time with Donovan and knows what he's like with girls." She shrugs. "Donovan's changed though. I've seen him a few times over this past week and he's different." She smiles. "I'm glad, Mara."

"Thanks." I turn to face her, "But what about you? What's going on?"

"I can't keep spending my time with a bunch of vipers. I'm sorry Mara, but I haven't done anything wrong and I'm not going to subject myself to them anymore." Her eyes meet mine before she averts them again. "I've tried, okay? I've tried for Reece, but I just can't anymore. I don't sleep that well at the best of times, but now it's so hard."

This isn't right. Surely my family can't be that bad. Well, apart from one person that is. Reece is going to go crazy when he finds out how she's been treated. I feel glee knowing he's going to go crazy at *her*. Kind of getting my own back. God, now I'm becoming Sarah. Ugh!

"Dahlia, I hear where you're coming from, but please think about Reece. He's your best friend and right now he's going crazy because he can't get in touch with you. He hasn't done anything to you, has he? It's my sister."

She nods her head swiping at a tear on her cheek. "I don't want Reece being upset with me, but, I don't feel strong enough to deal with it all today."

This is so not like her. My brother has led me to believe that she's a fighter and not someone to let people walk all over her.

"Dahlia, what's really going on?"

She won't look at me.

"Is it Sarah who's being a pain in the ass?"

She doesn't say anything but she flinches when I say her name.

"It is. If it's any consolation, she's being a bitch to me as well, and I have no idea why. I'm presuming it has something to do with Donovan, but I'm not all that sure."

"She hates me. She blames me for all the trouble between your mom and dad, and she won't leave me alone. She's like a toothache. The only reason I'm not doing or saying anything is because

she's Reece's sister. I don't want him to hate me."
She sounds lost.

"She's your sister too," I remind her so she
knows that she has family. "Reece won't hate you
for putting Sarah in her place. I mean I'm so close to
smacking her it isn't funny."

She laughs, but I'm not convinced she's telling
me everything, so I ask, "Are you sure that's it? I
mean we're talking about Reece's wedding here?"

Now she won't meet my eyes.

"Dahlia, please talk to me. I promise I'll keep it
to myself if that's what you want."

After a few minutes of silence, she whispers,
"Please call me Dal, and she's blackmailing me."
She sighs. "If I stay away from Reece and the rest of
you, she'll keep her mouth shut about something."

Wow. I wasn't expecting that.

"I just want Reece to have an amazing wedding
day without your sister spoiling it because of me. I'd
never forgive myself if it was ruined because I
called her bluff."

"What the hell is she blackmailing you with?"

"It isn't as big as you're thinking, but to Reece it
probably will be."

"Tell me."

She sighs. "You won't say anything?" She asks.

"I promise."

"About six months ago, I was in the wrong place at the wrong time. I'd had an argument with Ryder. He'd accused me of being a whore. I was upset and pissed so I'd gone off with a couple of girls who were passing through and we ended up meeting some guys they knew. I knew I shouldn't have gone with them, but I did. We ended up drinking and I did some drugs with them and finally passed out. When I woke up I got the hell out of there."

I sure as hell wasn't expecting that. As I watch Ryder join Donovan on the back steps, I try to think of something to say. My brother will be pissed she did the drugs, but surely if he knows the whole situation that stemmed from her argument with Ryder. But they seem to be friends now.

"How does Sarah know about it?"

"She was home for the weekend, and apparently gone shopping with a friend and spotted us."

I run my hands through my hair. "Look, my advice is to go to see Reece now. I'll come with you. You can tell him yourself. Tell him how you told me so he knows the whole thing. It isn't as bad as you think it is. I know what he's like about drugs—to the point he's obsessed, but if *you* tell him, you take away Sarah's hold, and I sure as hell can't wait to rub it in her face."

"Mara, she's your sister."

"Huh, so are you."

"Good point." She laughs.

"You haven't done drugs since, have you?"

"Hell no! That's the only time I've ever touched them. God, I was so sick the following day."

"Okay. We can go and see him now before he comes looking for you himself."

I link my arm with hers as we both stand and walk toward the waiting guys.

"So you made up with Ryder?"

"Yes and no."

"That isn't an answer."

"I know. I'm not sure what's going on with him. We haven't been intimate. I think he's lonely and decided I'll do as a friend because he's lacking."

"He's cute." I nudge her hip with mine.

She nudges me back. "No, he isn't."

"He's hot." I shove her harder this time.

"He's just a friend."

"Hmm. I'll let you off the hook for now, but only because we're going to talk to my brother, our brother." I grin. "We need to take your stuff over to my house once we've spoken to Reece. You can get ready in my room and Mom says we're going last at getting our hair put up."

"You're bossy for eighteen."

"I get it from Reece. I seriously can't wait to see

Sarah's face when you show up. I've never been close to her, but since we've been home this time, it's as though a switch has been turned on."

"Perhaps something's going on in her life, which is making her such a bitch to everyone else."

I've thought of that, but I really don't know anymore. I just want to forget about her and the trouble she's causing. My brother is getting married and I've got the sexiest guy in town as my *boyfriend*. So I'm going to concentrate on those two things instead of the doom and gloom from now on, although I'm going to end up saying something to her sooner rather than later because I have a problem keeping my mouth shut.

21

DONOVAN

"You've got it bad," Ryder smirks.

"I'm not the only one," I grin.

I do have it bad for Mara, and anyone looking at me when I'm watching her is going to know just how bad. She's really is 'my everything' and tonight I'm going to treat her like a princess. The scented candles are bought and already laid out around my bedroom ready to be lit. They are cinnamon scented ones because that's one of the only scents she likes. She says it reminds her of Christmas, her favorite time of year. So who am I to disappoint.

Much to my embarrassment, there is also a pot of strawberry massage oil hidden in my bedside drawer along with an unopened box of condoms. Hopefully we won't need those thanks to the injection she's had. I just want to be prepared in case she wants me to suit up because I'm not sure I'll survive not being inside her this time.

"Yep, really bad," Ryder says, climbing to his feet and wrapping Dahlia up in his arms.

"Are you okay?"

She nods her head and steps clear of him.

Ryder frowns.

"We need to go and see Reece. Can you take us there?" Mara asks me.

"Sure." I'm not sure how Reece will take me turning up with two of his sisters, but I'm not about to leave them to walk when my truck is right out front.

"Dal—"

"I'll be fine Ryder. I'm going to tell Reece about what happened with Mara there for backup." She gives him a hug but he keeps his hands on her when she pulls back. "I'll see you later at the wedding. You're still coming, right?" She asks biting her lip, and I grin when I see Ryder's eyes darken at the move. He's going down and I hope I'm around to witness it when he does.

"Donovan, c'mon we're running out of time. We have about an hour before we have to get back to my house to get ready for the wedding."

"Don't worry," I wrap my arm around her neck

and pull her into my body, needing this contact with her. "I'll have you both back with time to spare." *I hope.*

"Why are you hiding out here?" Jack asks standing beside me.

"More importantly what are you doing out here? Don't you have a bride to get ready for?"

"Stop changing the subject. What's really going on?"

I let out a sigh. "Something is going on with Dahlia. She's in there with Reece and Mara. I think Mara's there for backup." He gives me the 'tell me more' look. "I seriously don't know anything. They had a private talk at Kix and then asked me to drive them here."

"He's going to find out before you tell him at this rate."

"I know."

I shove my hands into my hair and tug, probably leaving it sticking up everywhere with the shit I've put in it to get it to behave for the guys' wedding pictures. Wiping my hands down the legs of my jeans to try and get the sticky stuff off, I hear Jack chuckle.

"We'll tell him after he's married. In a couple of days, when he gets back from his couple of nights away with his new wife." I grin.

"Yeah, he should be mellow by then." Jack looks back toward the door. "How long have they been in there?"

"About thirty minutes."

He shakes his head. "I'm heading back." He starts to move away. "You have an hour to be ready."

Shit!

"I'll be ready."

I watch him go before heading toward the door of the cabin Reece and Callie have been staying in since they got back here. Whatever they are discussing in there needs hurrying along. I've no idea how long it's going to take Mara and Dahlia to get ready, but they need to get a move on.

Making a louder noise than usual, I open the door and walk in and see Mara standing up to her brother, who is practically nose-to-nose with her. My first instinct is to go and pull her behind me—to protect my girl.

"You're a dick," she fumes at him.

My girl sure has a way with words, but I don't think Reece would agree with that right now. His eyes narrow as he gets closer to her.

Okay, I'm stepping in because I can't stand here

and watch him get pissed at her. I know he won't hurt her, but he still looks threatening, which I can't handle when its directed at Mara. What I can't understand is where has Dahlia disappeared to, and why isn't he mad at her instead of Mara. What the hell has Mara said to get him worked up?

They're so distracted with each other that they haven't seen me yet, but as I step in close to Mara, Reece raises his eyes to look at me. Mara whips around and stumbles against me. Reaching out, I help her stay steady by wrapping an arm around her. She shivers at my touch and it takes everything in me not to haul her against me and ravish her mouth. With great reluctance, I pull my eyes from her and meet Reece's gaze above her head. Okay, this isn't the best move I've ever made.

"Take your hands off my sister," he growls.

"What the fuck, Reece." Mara whirls back around and stomps on her brother's foot.

I grin, but pick her up and put her behind me. "Why are you pissed at Mara?"

"He's pissed at me, and taking it out on Mara," Dahlia says coming back into the room. "She has nothing to do with this. She's here because she persuaded me to tell you the truth."

Reece is like a bull in a fuckin' china shop sometimes, and doesn't think things through before he

190

reacts—like now. He shakes his head and I see the anger fade away in his eyes before he runs his hand over his face. He has definitely calmed himself down and it's clear in his tone. "Fuck. I'm sorry, Mara, but I'm not going to be sorry for what I say to *Sarah*. She's causing too much trouble for me to sit back and say nothing."

"That's fine."

What the hell has she done now? I know she's trying to interfere between Mara and me, but Dahlia as well, that's just plain crazy.

Right now though, especially since it looks like everything is solved between Reece and Dahlia, I need to get them back. "Okay, girls, I need to get you both over to the house to get ready. We're running out of time."

"Let's go," Mara says, stepping around me to hug Reece. "It's your wedding today so please forget about this for now. Callie won't forgive you if you screw this up with that temper of yours."

"Don't worry, I'll put it on hold."

Reece hugs Dahlia as well before shoving everyone out the door. I usher them to my truck and feel my heart sink when Mara climbs in the back. Dahlia hesitates, but climbs into the front mumbling about something I don't quite catch.

Turning out of sight from the cabin, Dahlia unclips and starts climbing into the back.

"Go sit up front with your guy," she tells Mara.

Within seconds, Mara is over into the front and pressed up against my side. I slide my fingers between hers and hold on tight to her hand.

We drive back to her house in silence and pulling up in front, I watch as Dahlia gets out and is called inside by Cindy. I climb out and pull Mara out through my door and into my arms. We're slightly sheltered from view by the door with the darkened glass, but anyone really looking will see how close our feet are beneath the truck.

I cup her face in my hands and meet her lips with mine. She moans and opens her mouth to me. As our tongues caress in wet heat, other parts of my body come alive and press against her stomach. She rubs against me causing an ache deep in my balls. One of my hands slides down her back to caress over her bottom. I press her into me and groan as my cock enlarges and leaks with excitement. Feeling her hard nipples against my chest isn't helping any, and it's making me want to rip her clothes off to taste her. Think her mom might have something to say about that though, at least while we're outside her house.

Breathing heavily, I place both hands on her hips and move her away from my aching body. "Tonight. Tonight I want you to stay with me. All night in my bed." Talking about tonight isn't helping to calm me down. Imagining her all warm and naked in my arms—wet and tight as I slide inside her—having her walls massage my length.

Groaning, I release her completely and rest against the side of the truck while I try to calm my body down.

"Are you okay?" she asks, rubbing my back.

"I'm fine, but please don't do that."

Her hand pauses on me.

"I want you like crazy and with you touching me, I'm so close to saying, to hell with this and shoving you back in to my truck and bringing tonight forward." I turn my head to look at her.

"Okay," she smiles, "I'll leave you alone for now, but promise me something."

I nod.

"Promise me that no matter what, you'll dance with me tonight at Reece and Callie's wedding."

Moving away from my truck, I lazily walk toward her, "How can I not," I quickly kiss her, "dance with my girl. Now go in there and get ready." I kiss her again. "I'll see you there."

"Okay. I miss you already," she shouts over her shoulder as she runs toward her house.

After she's gone back inside, I climb into my truck and pulling away I'm wishing my life away to this evening to when I'll have Mara to myself. I only hope I survive.

22

MARA

As soon as I walk inside my home, the chaos hits me. Both Callie and Thalia are getting ready here, which also means both sets of parents are here somewhere, probably hiding out in the lounge. My four sisters look to be nearly ready with their hair and make-up sorted. Even with all the business, I catch Sarah glaring at me across the room.

She will have seen Dal here or at least seen her on the way to my room. Letting out a loud sigh, which has Jessie and Robin looking my way. I ignore them and walk toward Sarah, taking hold of her wrist as I pull her out of the room with me and toward the downstairs' coat closet.

Opening the door and dragging her inside, I

slam the door shut and standing in front of her, I try to catch my breath. I don't want to start a shouting match with her, but my need to keep the peace for Reece and Callie today is making me say something to her when in reality I'd rather avoid her.

"Look Sarah, I've no idea what's wrong with you but you need to stop pissing everyone off. Reece knows all about what you had over Dahlia," her eyes widen, "because she told Reece not too long ago. So can we please try and all get along, at least for today? Reece is pissed, but I'm sure if he can hold off so can you."

She narrows her eyes at me and takes a step forward. "Why Mara? Why did you take Donovan away from me? He's mine. He's always been mine, but you, my sister, have taken him away from me. You're a whore and I hate you."

She grabs the door handle and shoving me, aside stomps out.

I'm left floundering. Whore? And what the fuck did she mean? He's always been hers. I very much doubt Donovan knows that.

She's crazy.

I wonder if she was adopted.

Both Callie and Thalia are glowing right now in their wedding finery. They have both gone for simple, but elegant. Thalia's dress is a fitted bodice with tiny beading creating flower patterns all over with a straight long skirt. Her skirt is long in the back to form a small train, but the front has a slit up to mid-thigh, which is going to give Jack something to think about when he catches sight of his bride.

I chuckle though when I catch sight of the white and silver cowgirl boots on her feet.

And then there is Callie, looking happy, but nervous in her white dress. Callie's dress is off one shoulder with beading like Thalia's, but that's where the similarity's end. Callie's dress is fitted to her curves and drops to the floor where I can see the toes of her red boots sticking out. I'd watched her pull them on. She had laughed and told me that Reece had a thing about her in her red, cowgirl boots so she'd figured she really would get his blood going today by wearing her new thigh high boots that Reece hasn't seen yet.

It was too much information really, but whatever. I can't wait to get around to the back of Jack's parents house to where Donovan will be standing with Reece. He's gorgeous in a suit, but in a tux, he's going to make me pant. And seeing four gorgeous guys standing together might make me feel light headed as well. Liam, Jack's brother is standing for him. So yeah, three hot guys and my brother.

"You ready?" Mia, Liam's wife asks.

"I am. I can't wait to see how everything looks and the guys in their tux."

She grins. "Oh, they look mighty fine. Liam's already had to dress twice," she smirks.

My eyes pop wide.

"Stop catching flies. I can't help it if I find my husband sexy in his tux. I've already been scouting for somewhere private for later because I'm not going to be able to wait." She grins and carries on, "I'm constantly horny at this time of month. Liam loves it."

"I bet he does."

I've known Mia for most of my life, but right about now she could do with a filter on her mouth.

Why does everyone keep giving me too much information today? I guess I better stay away from Aunt Betty who has no sensor whatsoever. God knows what she'll come out with.

"Girls, come on. Get into position, we're about to go." Callie and Thalia link their arms with their fathers.

I'm walking behind them, but my eyes are on

the vast amount of flowers that are covering anything and everything. Hopefully, there won't be anyone with a bad case of allergies because this would start it up.

As we start walking down the makeshift aisle, I look around at friends and family who are here today smiling at the girls, the brides, and us, the bridesmaids. I have a smile on my face, which is starting to feel as though its plastered on, but then I catch sight of Donovan standing tall and proud next to Reece with eyes only for me.

He makes my heart thud in my chest with the possessive look he's throwing at me. Because I'm walking behind Callie, he hasn't seen the dress I'm wearing, which I chose with him in mind. The dress flows down to my feet in a soft lemon silk with a slit up my right thigh to my waist. Beneath though I'm wearing matching lemon shorts and they are *short* too. The whole outfit reminds me of the fifty's fashion except the top part of the dress is a fitted strapless bodice, which dips low between my large breasts. Even Liam did a double take when he saw me in it before looking away.

Coming to a stop near Donovan, his eyes widen as he takes me in before I notice his jaw visibly tighten and his fist clench.

Mission accomplished!

While the justice of the peace starts with his wedding talk, instead of listening I spend my time casting sly glances at my man. He really is so handsome in his tux. The white shirt really stands out against his dark sun kissed skin, which my tongue is itching to lick.

Licking along my lips, I catch his eyes as they darken with passion watching me. I stick my tongue out and watch as his lust filled eyes widen in shock before narrowing.

Feeling a prod in my back, I turn and glare at Sarah, who is standing behind me with a matching glare.

"Stop looking at him," she hisses between her teeth.

What a bitch!

Really hating myself, I do as she says because the last thing I want is for her to cause problems right now. I don't think I've felt like punching anyone the way I do right now, and she's my sister, which is kind of sad.

Before I know it, both Reece and Jack are kissing their brides and everyone is cheering. Reece turns and hugs me tight, kissing me on the forehead before moving along to our sisters. He reluctantly hugs Sarah, but quickly lets her go before going back to his bride and doing a 'man hug' with Liam, Donovan and Jack.

Donovan looks at me with a frown on his face and I try to tell him with my eyes that it's because of Sarah. I don't think he gets it though, but as the brides and grooms take their place to walk down the aisle, Sarah sidles up next to Donovan who looks startled. His eyes meet mine over the top of Sarah's head.

I'm frozen in place not knowing whether to shove her out of the way or to keep my mouth shut and hands to myself. But she's pushing the limits with me now. Donovan is my guy and I'm going to fight for him if that's what she wants.

Seeing Sarah's distraction with Mom talking to her, I slip behind Robin, and slide my hand into Donovan's. With a slight tug, he's now standing beside me with a crooked grin on his handsome face.

"You're asking for trouble," he whispers against my ear causing a shiver to run straight down my spine to my pussy.

"As long as you're the trouble then it's fine with me." I press my chest briefly against his arm and hear his breath rush out through his lips when he feels my erect nipples.

He leans down to say something else when we both spot Sarah fuming in front of us.

Oh what fun.

"Ignore her babe. Don't let her ruin today for you."

"It's not me I'm bothered about."

"I know. C'mon. Let's follow everyone out. I think we have some photographs to crash," he says grinning.

23

DONOVAN

My balls are so tight to my body right now that I'm frightened to move. Mara has completely blown me over in the hot-as-fuck dress that she's wearing, and now while she's dancing with an uncle, I can't take my eyes from her breasts, which are swaying gently as she moves.

We sat opposite each other during the meal, which didn't go down too well with Mara, but for me I felt relief although it was short lived. Every time I glanced in her direction she was doing something suggestive. Whether it was eating a breadstick or sucking on the spoon with the sorbet on its tip. But little does she know that I'm planning on getting my own back on her tonight with a slow seduction. At least that's the plan, but with how much she's teasing me, I'm not sure I'm going to last to make it slow.

"You look ready to burst," Liam comments sitting next to be me.

"You have no idea," I mumble against my longneck.

"Little Mara sure has grown up. Even though there's only one woman for me I still had to do a double take earlier. Thought I was seeing things." Liam shakes his head. "And if I'm not mistaken, she's done nothing but look in this direction since she's been on the dance floor. You should go up there and ask her to dance."

I watch her from beneath my lashes, and without taking my eyes from her, I reply to Liam, "That's not such a good idea. Reece would flip."

"Reece isn't here. He worked out during the meal what kind of boots Callie is wearing so he's spent the rest of the time trying to work out how to get a look up her dress." He grins. "They're in the barn."

On his wedding day as well, but then, if you can't fuck your bride in the barn on your wedding day then there isn't much hope for you.

"Donovan for fuck's sake, get up there before someone else snaps her up when it's you she really wants."

I don't need telling twice.

My feet have a mind of their own as I watch Derek from the car place in town about to make his move on her. *I don't think so buddy.*

Moving in quickly, I slide my arm around Mara's waist and turn her in my arms. Her whole face lights up when she realizes it's me. Her arms wrap around my neck as I fit her snug against me. Not an inch between us.

"I missed you," she whispers against my ear just before I feel her tongue swirl around my lobe.

"Behave." I press her tight against me and groan when she does a slight rotate with her hips against my hard dick.

The music changes to Emeli Sandé, Beneath You are Beautiful. Hardly moving, we gently sway around the dance floor. My objective is to escape through the marquee's back entrance to have a private five minutes with my girl. God knows I deserve it. I kept my distance after we walked backed down the aisle together. It was either that or kidnap her for the rest of the day.

Feeling her body gently moving against mine is driving me insane. The feel of her curves in my hands is causing my body to tighten with suppressed need. The lust that is roaring through me makes me certain that I'm going to have to jerk off in the bathroom before I take her back to my place. Tonight I need to go slower than I've ever gone before to show her how much she means to me—how special she is to me—how much I *love* her.

Finally seeing the exit close, I grab her bottom in my hands and smile when I hear the moan escape her lips and feel her hands tighten at the nape of my neck. "Hold tight. We're leaving for a few minutes."

Quickly exiting with Mara, I look around for a private spot. Not finding anywhere other than the start of the trees, which separate the property from the river, I pick her up in my arms and carry her a few feet into the dense foliage for cover.

Placing her back on her feet, she takes hold of my face and brings me down to her for a hot, wet kiss. Her lips are soft and pliant under mine and as my tongue caresses hers, the taste of chocolate hits my taste buds. I deepen the kiss for more. I don't think I'll ever be able to get enough of this girl who I've given my heart to.

She breaks from the kiss and starts placing tiny kisses along my jaw as her hands pull my shirt free of my slacks. Her hands are everywhere, fluttering over my chest and abs, caressing over my ass, and, *fuck,* stroking along my dick, which jerks and lengthens. I've been on a tight rope all day so there's no way I'm going to stay loaded if she keeps touching and caressing my length.

Pulling her hand away, I meet her gaze. "I want you too badly to have you touching me there."

My eyes drop down to the gap between her breasts, which is bare thanks to the design of the dress. I dip down with my head and rub my nose along her collarbone, feeling her hands as they slide into my hair. "You have driven me crazy all day. Every time you moved, I could see your beautiful breasts sway slightly and I thought they'd be slipping out of your dress."

She groans as I rub my face over one of her erect nipples through her dress. "I knew they wouldn't fall out."

Going back to the gap in her dress, I nuzzle it open and nibble on the side of her breast while rubbing her neglected one with my fingers through the dress. She feels and tastes so damn hot.

As she moves against me, my dick is ready to break through the zipper to make contact with her rubbing pussy. And then my balls draw tight to my body. I quickly put her away from me and try to breathe.

Mara takes one look at me before letting her eyes travel down my body to hover around my groin area. She licks her lips and starts to get to her knees.

I can't let her do this. I want her to do this.

"Wait."

"Donovan, you can't go anywhere like that. I want you in my mouth."

"Fuck. Here." I quickly remove my jacket and drop it to the ground.

She hitches her dress up and kneels on my crumpled jacket before grinning up at me.

"I'm going to come as soon as you touch me," I warn.

"Wait until you're in my mouth."

My head drops back against the tree trying to shut out her words and the picture of her on her knees.

Her hands slide up my thighs, landing on my zipper, which she pulls down really slow. I bite my lip to keep the groan inside.

Shoving her hands inside my shorts on my ass she shoves them and my slacks down my legs in one swift move, letting my huge dick burst free against her face.

My groan escapes as she turns slightly and captures my erection with her tongue and licks from root to tip where she swirls her tongue around the head. Lapping up all the pre-cum, which won't stop leaking out in my excitement.

Her hand cups my balls and starts a gentle massage as she sucks the tip into her mouth. My legs shake and the blood thrums through my body getting ready to detonate.

I've needed to release all evening and, *fuck!* "Babe. Oh God. I'm going—fuck."

Exploding in her mouth while she's sucking me is the hottest, most arousing thing ever. My orgasm is going on and on. My cock jerks, releasing more cum the more she sucks me off. I can't take it any more so I try and pull away from her, but she grabs my ass and keeps me against her.

"Babe, let go. No more," I groan. My cocks only slightly shrunk with my release, but it won't take much to get me to full arousal again with her mouth.

She backs away slightly, and holding the root of me starts licking me clean as my dick starts to lengthen again. "Mara, babe. Please stop. We can't stay out here all night and if you keep doing that I'm still not going to be able to walk." She lets me go with a sexy grin on her lips. "Fuck, you make me act like a sixteen year old."

Holding my hand out to her, I haul her to her feet and kiss her. My scent is still on her as the kiss deepens making me dizzy. Feeling my cock swell between us, I put her away from me and hitch my shorts and slacks back up around my hips, needing everything covered and contained for now.

"I take it you enjoyed that?" she asks, knowing damn well I enjoyed what she did to me.

"Damn straight I did. Your turn soon, baby." I cup her face and kiss her then have to force myself to let her go when all I want is to keep her by my side.

"We better head back before we're missed, if we're not already."

"I have a feeling if we are that Liam will cover for us."

"Liam?" she questions as I take her hand and start to lead her back to the marquee, not really bothered if anyone sees us.

"Yeah. I kind of gave my feelings away when you were out on the dance floor." I offer her a wry smile.

"Hmm. I don't mind if it makes you react like that again."

Chuckling, I release her hand and sneak inside the marquee behind her.

24

MARA

Spotting my brother and Callie ahead of us, I squeeze Donovan's hand to get his attention and indicate to him that I'll see him later. It hurts to have to separate from him especially after what I've just done to him, and the further away I walk, the closer I feel to tears.

"Mara, come and talk to me." Mia takes my arm and pulls me over to a quiet corner of the marquee, if you can call any area quiet with the music blasting our eardrums. In fact, if I'm not mistaken the guys are supposed to be getting on the make shift stage to serenade their wives soon, and I'm going to pretend that Donovan is serenading me.

"Why are you upset? I don't remember you spending any time with Sarah."

She makes me smile. "I've stayed well away from her today." My smile slips. "It's just that it hurts having to stay apart for now when I want to be close to him." I swipe a tear from my face and look in the direction Donovan disappeared in and catch his gaze. He looks concerned when he notices the tears I'm unable to hide, but I shake my head and hope he stays where he is.

"Oh Mara, it will all work out. Reece and Callie are going away for two nights, right? So while they're gone you can be together and then as soon as they get back you need to tell them before someone else does."

"I know. If I know my luck, Sarah will get to him beforehand anyway." I shrug. "She is suffering from a major case of PMS." I smile. "I'll be fine. Please don't worry about me. He has a very romantic night planned for my first time tonight, and I'm hoping I'll be spending the next few nights with him as well."

"Good for you, um, you know about things right?"

I'd just taken a gulp of the wine she shoved in to my hands, which I'm underage for, but what the hell when she asked me that. Do I shock her or embarrass her?

Leaning in to her, she leans in closer to me and

waits. It's killing me keeping a frown on my face. "I may still be a virgin, but we've seen each other naked before and we may or may not have fooled around." I grin at the wide-eyed stare she throws my way. "Mia, you're looking at me as though you never fooled around with Liam, which we both know isn't true."

"Wow. Sorry. You look young, sweet and innocent. So tell me, is he hot beneath his clothes?" She laughs.

"Just curious. Liam's enough man for me and he has muscle and size in all the right places, if you know what I mean." She winks.

"Donovan's sexy and delicious and I can't get enough of him. I've waited a long time for him to notice me, well maybe not notice as he admits to noticing me just fine, but for him to make his move. I guess it helped with me moving to the city to where they are, but I just feel that we're counting down to the bomb going off, you know? Reece isn't going to be happy at all."

"Reece will have to be happy. Don't let him ruin this for you. I know he's your brother, but he doesn't always know what's best for you. Plus he has Callie now so she'll be on your side."

"I know. I'll be glad when it's all out in the open. I hate hiding." Turning away, I cringe. I've been hiding for years with my blog, although this is different.

"It's time," Mia says and points to the dance floor.

Turning in my seat, I watch the guys take to the stage with Jack adjusting the microphone. Even though Jack tends to lead with the singing, they all have good strong voices. I'll never forget the time Mrs. O'Leary's husband died. He was ninety-two and had a soft spot for Reece, which was returned. So she'd asked if him, Donovan and Jack would sing Amazing Grace at his funeral. They had and there wasn't a dry face in the church by the time they'd finished.

And now watching Reece and Donovan move their microphones inline with Jack, I realize I should have been prepared and grabbed a couple of napkins. Whatever they are planning to sing, they don't seem to be planning on using their instruments.

My hearts pounding already and they haven't even started.

Jack taps the microphone to grab everyone's attention. "I'm not going to bore you all with another speech. But I do need to say that although I've written a song especially for today that isn't what we're going to be singing tonight. Instead we are going to sing something that I could probably sing in my sleep because Thalia along with Callie have watched the movie that it goes with so many times we've lost count."

Everyone starts laughing. I know what he's talking about because I've watched it a few times with Callie back at the apartment and she sobs at the same place every time. *Titanic.*

"This is for our girls."

And then, just wow. They start singing My Heart Will Go On, and I don't have the words to describe how amazing they sound. They don't sing like this anymore—not for a long time, but they are amazing. They should do this more often.

My gaze flicks to Jack and Reece, but it's Donovan who keeps his gaze on me while he sings. He is just beautiful. They all are. Standing there in their black slacks, white shirts, ties undone that are dangling down in front of their chests and their jackets. My heart pounds as they put everything they have into this song, which they've obviously been practicing. As the song nears the end, the urge to go to Donovan and slide my hands up his chest is becoming unbearable. Thalia and Callie are standing in front of their guys, wiping tears from their cheeks as their guys finish the most beautiful song I've ever heard them sing.

The brides are in their husband's arms while Donovan slips off to the side clenching his fists. I see my mom move over to him and I'm not sure what she's saying, but he looks toward me before turning back to her.

Mia notices my distraction and pulls me around to face her. "Stop. I can see the worry on your face."

I'm trying to shake myself out of whatever I've fallen into, when I'm nudged from behind.

"They're throwing their bouquets. In the foyer," Robin shouts to us as she races out the marquee.

"C'mon, let's go."

"You're already married," I point out the obvious as Mia drags me up from the table.

"I can still have some fun at your expense. You have to catch one of them Mara, and I can't wait to see Donovan's face when you do."

As Mia ushers me along with everyone into the foyer of Jack's parents house, I ask, "You do realize I'm not the only unwed girl here?"

"Of course I do." She grins.

What does she have planned?

I glance at her again and she's still grinning. She's up to something.

"Here, stand right there." She maneuvers me into a spot. "Do not consider moving."

"Do you know something, I don't?"

216

"Maybe."

I'm about to reply when I spot Donovan leaning against the wall with a sexy grin on his face.

"Oh my god, he has it just as bad as you do. Look at his grin."

"I'm looking."

"Then again you need to look ahead."

Mia sounds so damn excited, you'd think she wasn't married.

"Why are you trying to catch that shit?" Liam asks.

"I'm not. Mara is."

He rolls his eyes at her excitement as she continues, "Make sure you reach for it Mara. Don't disappoint me."

I grin. "Yes ma'am."

"Wait," Callie shouts from the top of the stairs. "Mara, get up here a minute."

What?

"Go," Mia gives me a shove to get me moving.

Conscience of all the wedding guests watching me walk upstairs, I really wish I'd taken my shoes off at the bottom because coming back down is going to be awkward.

Reaching Callie, she takes my hands into hers and pulls me close. "If you don't catch this, I'm not going to be impressed."

"Are you serious?" I look at her incredulous.

"Of course I am."

"God, between you and Mia I'm sure I'm going to manage. Just make sure you throw it in my direction. Now can we get on with it? Everyone is watching."

She grins. "Yeah go, and make sure you stand near where Donovan is right now."

"Okay."

I turn and try to ignore the stares, which make me feel uncomfortable. Being center of attention isn't me and stresses me out.

As I put my right foot forward, I feel a crack and then I start to stumble. My heel breaks. Reaching out, my hand connects with fresh air as I completely loose my balance and start falling down the stairs. My head cracks against the wall, my legs bash into the bannister and my arm—the pain. The last thing I hear is Donovan shouting my name.

25

DONOVAN

WATCHING MARA LOSE HER BALANCE ON THE stairs and then proceed to fall the rest of the way down has taken ten years off my life. I'm sure.

Screaming her name, I push through the guests in the foyer just needing to get to my girl. Right now I don't give a shit who knows or finds out about us because I need to be there with her.

Breaking through everyone, I freeze. Mara is in a heap at the bottom of the stairs, unmoving. I drop to my knees by her head and smooth the hair from her face before dropping my forehead to hers. She blurs as my eyes fill with unshed tears. "Baby, please wake up," I whisper to her. "I need you Mara."

"Mara. Jesus. Fuck. Get the paramedics," Reece

shouts to the room at large. "Is she breathing?" he asks.

I raise my head knowing the minute he sees my face, he'll know I'm in love with her. There's no hiding it.

"She's breathing," I say meeting his gaze and watch as his eyes widen.

"Mara," Cindy, her mom cries. She sits on the floor beside me, but I think it has more to do with her legs not managing to hold her up anymore. "Please tell me my baby is okay."

"I don't," my voice cracks, "know. I wish I did."

She wraps her arm around my shoulders. "She's strong. She'll be okay. She has to be, I need you both to give me grandchildren one day."

"What the fuck," Reece cusses.

"Now isn't the time," I croak as the paramedics arrive. I thank God that they were close by with a quick response time.

"Yeah, but—"

"Reece." Callie pulls him up and into her arms. He holds her while she cries softly into his chest.

Dropping my gaze, I ask one of the paramedics, "Will she be okay?"

"Her right arms looks to be broken. Not too sure about her legs. We're going to put a collar on her and make her as comfortable as we can to transport her to the hospital."

I nod in acknowledgement.

My legs feel like jelly when Jack pulls me up from the floor. "What do you need?" he asks.

"Mara." I'm struggling with my emotions. He wraps his arms around me and just holds me tight. I grab on to the back of his jacket needing his support right now. All I can see is Mara tumbling down the stairs and feel the fear of losing her in my chest.

"She's going to be all right."

I nod and pull away from him as the paramedics start to move her.

"There's enough room for one in the ambulance with us."

I stay frozen to the floor when realization hits— I'm not going to be able to stay with her. Her mom will be going. There's no reason why I should feel hurt that I won't be going with her, but I do. I don't ever want to leave her.

Feeling hands on my arm, I turn and face her mom. She cups my face in her hands and says, "You go with her." I shake my head. *She's her mom.* "Yes. I'm going to follow, but you need to be with her. It's you she'll want to see when she comes around. No arguing. Just go and get in the ambulance with her."

Not needing telling twice, I ignore the glare

Reece is throwing in my direction and shoot out of the door to follow them.

Staring out of the window on the third floor of the hospital, I don't really see anything. All my thoughts are about Mara and wondering what the hell they are doing that's taking so damn long to assess her. We've been here about an hour now and the not knowing is driving me crazy.

Mara's mom, sisters and brother arrived within minutes of us arriving and we seem to have taken over the waiting room here at the hospital. Reece is keeping his distance from me, which is a good thing right now, but I'd rather have him by my side than miles away.

Jack is here with Thalia, and had to pull his new wife away from me not too long ago. I appreciate her wanting to comfort me, but the only one I want close to me is Mara and that isn't going to happen any time soon.

It kills me that she's suffering alone and doesn't have anyone in there with her—holding her hand.

"The Kincaid family?"

Turning, a guy in scrubs is addressing the room at large, and my heart stops. What if she isn't going to be okay? How the fuck am I going to handle that?

I stay where I am, but the guy starts talking too quietly for me to hear so I walk toward them and hear him mention surgery.

"Why does she need surgery?"

He pauses as if undecided whether or not to talk.

"It's okay," Cindy says, "he's family."

Reece stays quiet but his eyes are filled with something I can't quite decipher.

"She's broken her arm in a couple of places and she needs to have a pin inserted in order for it to mend quickly, and now I need to get back to her, but is someone named Donovan here?"

"That's me."

"Follow me, she keeps asking for you."

"When can we see her?" Reece asks.

"We're getting her ready for the surgery so when she's come round and been transferred to her own room, but she's only started cooperating with us after I promised to come and find Donovan. She's basically refusing the surgery until she's seen him."

"Me and you are having words once she's okay," Reece growls.

I'm sure it's only Callie's presence that's preventing him from starting anything with me right now, and for that I'm thankful. The last thing Mara needs is to see her brother and myself a bit worse for wear because of our fists.

I nod at him and then follow the doctor through the doors to go to my girl.

Walking into the room, she has my heart beating franticly in my chest. She's smiling at me. How can she smile at me while obviously in so much pain?

The longer I stand staring at her, the smile she has on her face just for me starts to slip, which gets my feet moving.

As soon as I'm close enough she grabs my hand and holds on tight. Tears form in her eyes, which probably match mine.

A nurse shoves me into a chair that she's just placed at the side of the bed. My knees were about to give way with relief anyway.

"I'm okay," she whispers.

Shaking my head, I drop my forehead to our joined hands on the bed by her hip and kiss her knuckles. Glancing up, I'm met with her watering eyes.

"I love you, Mara," I smile, "and it nearly killed me watching you fall."

"You love me?"

Offering a wry smile, I reply, "Yeah, I do. I've been in love with you for two years. I've tried to fight my feelings for you, but you're inside me and you're not going to move—ever. Before this past week, the memory that always sticks in my head from back then was that hot summer when you turned sixteen. It was hotter than usual, and Reece had gotten the water guns out. I remember you, Robin and some of your friends were in shorts and bikini tops running around while Reece, Jack and me were attacking with the water guns. You'd disappeared from sight, but after looking around, I'd spotted you sneaking around the side of the house so I'd gone and snuck up on you. Except as I ran around the corner, I smacked into you and lost my balance, taking us both down to the ground with you on top of me. I looked into your eyes and seeing the tears in your eyes, I'd been lost. My heart has been yours since that exact moment. It had scared the shit outta me, but not anymore."

"A wonderful memory. Thank you for telling me that. I can't wait for this to be over with so you can hold me close, because I really need your arms around me."

Standing up, I caress her cheeks with my thumbs as I lean over and kiss her on the lips. "I love you baby, and I'll be here when you wake up. Okay?"

"I love you too. Always."

I kiss her again when I see a couple of nurses coming toward us. My heart is going into a panic at having to leave her while she goes down to the OR. My need to stay with her is so strong that I'm not sure I'm going to be able to walk back to the waiting room—not able to let go of her hand.

"We need to take her down now." A nurse tells me. "She'll be okay. Why don't you go back to the waiting room and someone will come down when she's awake."

I kiss her one last time, and whisper how much I love her before I watch them wheel her away from me. It feels like she's taking my heart with her—as though someone is physically ripping it out of my chest. It hurts. It hurts a lot. I need to get out of here before I completely fall to pieces.

Ignoring the stares around me as I weave in and out of the corridor, I push through the doors at the end and stop. Reece, her mom and everyone else who is there waiting for news on Mara is looking at me. I don't know what to say. I'm not even sure if I tried to say something that anything would come out of my mouth.

Her mom, Cindy, walks over to me and takes

my face between her hands and gazes into my eyes. I'm pretty sure she can see how wrecked I am right now. Out of the corner of my eye, I spot Reece moving in closer and realize they all need to know how Mara is. I was able to see her, but her family hasn't.

"She's okay—" my voice breaks.

"Oh honey, come here." Her mom pulls me into her and holds me while I cry.

I'm a guy. I don't cry, but I am now. The first time since my parents died. I guess the shock of everything is catching up to me, as well as relief that she's going to be okay, when she could have been so easily taken away from me.

"She's a tough one, Donovan. She'll be okay, and in a day or two she'll be pissing everyone off because she'll be laid up on bed rest."

I smile at her mom's attempt to help me. It's working as well. Inhaling and exhaling, I slowly pull away from her and take the napkins Callie passes to me. "Thanks."

"Will you be okay?"

"I'll be okay when Mara's out of surgery."

Glancing at Reece, I can't read his thoughts. He's usually so open and easy to read, but now he's wearing his poker face.

I need to escape if only for five minutes to catch

my breath and regroup the best I can for when she comes out of surgery. I promised her that I'd be here when she does and nothing and no one is going to make me break that promise. I'd be there with her, even if I hadn't promised because she's my *everything*.

"I'll be back in a minute." I quickly head to the restroom and lean on the sink, letting my head drop down with my eyes closed. I need a few minutes to pull myself together before she's back from there.

"She'd be upset if she knew you were falling to bits worrying about her."

Straightening, I turn and face Reece not knowing how the hell he's going to react to my relationship with his sister. I owe him an apology as well, but I'm not sure I'm ready to give it. I'm not really ready for this either.

"How long?" he asks, his voice level. He doesn't sound pissed—yet.

"I'm not sure what you're asking me. How long have I been with your sister or how long have I been in love with her?"

He frowns. "You love her?"

"I've been in love with her for the past couple of years," I shove my hands into my hair, "but we've only been together this past week. I've tried so damn hard to stay away from her and until she

228

moved to the city I thought I was okay." I laugh. "But you know Mara. She always goes after what she wants and she's decided that it's me she wants." My voice cracks again.

"When were you planning on telling me," he asks, moving closer.

I'm not afraid of him. We've been friends for too many years for him to frighten me, but the thought of our friendship suffering causes a pain in my chest.

"When you got back from your two nights away with Callie. None of us wanted to spoil your wedding by pissing you off. I'm not sorry for being with her. I've told you I love her—that's the truth, but I am sorry we decided to wait to tell you. No matter how you would have reacted you deserved to know."

"Yeah, I did—*Fuck*—I want to be pissed as fuck with you, but, with everything that's happened and your reaction, I can't get there."

I splash my face with water to hopefully cover up my grin at his admission.

"Don't be a dick." He shoves me. "I can't get my head around the fact that you're having, um, you know with my baby sister."

"Sex?"

He scowls.

"Don't tell her I told you this, but I haven't fu—um, been inside her yet." That was a close call, but perhaps I should have left off "yet."

Raising an eyebrow, he glares at me. I've caught him by surprise.

"You're telling me that you haven't messed about? You haven't made a move on her?"

Shaking my head, I grab some paper napkins and dry off before replying, "I'm not sure what you want me to say because I'm certainly not telling you what we've done, but I can assure you she's still intact. Her first time is going to be slow and special, not quick and brutal. What do you take me for?"

"Fuck. I knew it was only a matter of time before you both hooked up."

"You did?" *Unbelievable.*

"Yeah, I did. She's only had eyes on you for years, and I've wondered about you with the looks you throw at her when you think no one is watching, and that mixed with you not wanting to hook up with anyone for longer than a night kinda made me think, you know?"

I seriously had no idea that I was so transparent.

"But what was all the 'stay away from my *baby* sister' about? That sounded pretty damn clear to me."

"Reverse psychology my friend or rather it has

been more so since that thing at the museum." He grins. "Although it was a shock seeing you with her back at the house after she'd fallen because I had no idea you were actually together."

"So let me get this right. All that about protecting your sister was a load of bullshit."

He leans a hip against the sink and faces me. "No it wasn't bullshit, but not wanting her to get with you was because I wanted you to work for her. I figured if you had to fight to get her you'd be more likely to keep her. Like Callie and me." He shrugs.

I didn't think I'd be smiling tonight at the hospital, but hearing him say that makes my heart lighter and I know it will Mara's. I could punch him for making us feel as though we shouldn't be together though.

"You're one of my best friends—like a brother to me. There isn't any reason why I wouldn't trust you with my sister, at least now. When she was sixteen I might have had something more to say about it, but not now. You needed to sweat before you got the girl." He grins.

"Fucker!"

26

MARA

Waking up slowly my whole body feels like it's broken and my throat feels as though someone has given me a spoon of sawdust. Even breathing hurts.

Without moving my neck, I glance out of the corner of my eye and see the machines, which are obviously monitoring me. Moving my eyes to the other side, I pause. Donovan is sitting in what looks to be a very uncomfortable chair, asleep, looking rumpled. *How long has he been here? How long have I been here?*

"Donovan," I barely manage to whisper.

I desperately need a drink.

Trying again, I croak, "Donovan."

He hears me this time and shoots up with a wince and quickly makes his way over to me.

"You're awake. Do you need anything?" He takes my fingers in his and strokes my thumb.

"Water."

"One minute."

Before I have time to think, he has a plastic cup with a straw in his hand.

"Take a sip."

Holding it to my mouth, he puts the straw between my lips and I take a slow drink, and then some more. I never thought I'd ever be so greedy for water, but I am now.

"Hey, guzzler. Slow down."

I release the straw from between my lips and let Donovan take my drink away. I test my voice now that it doesn't feel so dry, "How long have I been asleep?"

"All night. You've been in and out of it really."

Donovan pulls a chair up to the side of the bed and takes my hand, pressing it against his cheek, which is coated in a sexy five o'clock shadow. "You look sexy, and tired."

"I'm exhausted, but I'll sleep when you're out of here."

"When?"

"The doc said all being well, he'll release you

tomorrow, but he wants to see how you're feeling first."

Caressing his face with my fingers, I slide them between his lips and feel the tip of his tongue make contact. My fingers tingle.

"Enough of that." Donovan takes hold of my wrist and places my hand back on the bed, but keeps his hand wrapped around me. "I can't stop touching you."

"Don't ever stop."

"I don't intend to." He lets out a long sigh and rests his head on the bed beside my hip, and closes his eyes. Poor guy is exhausted. Reaching out, I gently caress his face and smile when he sighs into my hand.

I'm so in love with this guy and knowing he loves me just as much makes my heart pound. He's a good guy, and he doesn't know it yet, but when I get out of here I'm moving in with him, well I hope I am. I guess it depends on how mobile I'm going to be because I don't want to dump my injured ass on him.

Feeling sleepy again, I start to drift off when the door in front of my bed starts to open. *Reece.*

Crap!

My eyes widen when he looks at me for what feels like hours, but are probably mere seconds before his eyes travel to Donovan, and then back to me..

"Don't panic," he whispers. "I know all about you and Donovan. Right now though I want to know how you're doing?" He comes over to the side of the bed next to Donovan and kisses me on my forehead with his arm resting above my head on the pillow as he stays close.

"I'm sore, but okay."

He's my big brother and I love him so much, which makes me feel guilty for doing this on his wedding day. "I'm sorry," I mumble and start crying. "I'm so sorry for ruining your wedding night."

"Shush. Mara. God. You didn't ruin anything, well apart from your dignity," he smirks, but I'm not fooled with the tears in his eyes. "You scared the ever living shit outta me, sis. If I ever catch you in heels again I'm going to pick you up and yank the damn things off. You got that."

"Yeah."

"She's sticking to her boots after this. I'll make sure of it," Donovan adds.

"I thought you were sleeping."

"I was." He scowls at Reece, who grins.

"How do you know about Donovan and me?" I ask needing to know whether Donovan told him or whether it was my trip down the stairs that had him realizing we had become more than friends.

"I'm not an idiot, Mara. Reverse psychology, and it worked a treat."

"I'm confused."

"I told you both to stay away from each other—reverse psychology."

Really!

"So you mean to tell me, all the time we were worried about how us being together would affect you, you wanted us together."

Reece grins.

"You're a dick," I point out.

"Yeah, but you love me."

"Hmm."

"Good morning. How's my patient today?" the nurse asks barging in as though there isn't two guys at the side of my bed.

"Okay, I think. My whole body feels as though I've been hit by an eighteen-wheeler, but can I ask what my injuries are?"

I should have asked Donovan, but he looked so ready to break that I'd wanted to spare his feelings and wait.

"That's what stumbling down stairs will do to you. The doctor operated on your arm last night and put a couple of pins in there to help it heal so you haven't to move it. A cast will be going on later today once the swelling has reduced a bit more. Your ankle is badly sprained so you're going to have trouble getting around for a while because we can't give you crutches with your arm like it is, although if you need it they might give you one crutch to help you balance."

"Wonderful. So I'm going to need help getting around? Is that what you're saying?"

"I'm afraid so, Honey." She straps the blood pressure cuff around my good arm now that the guys have stepped over to the window for her to do her job. "Don't worry. You'll be back on your feet in no time providing you don't put any pressure on your ankle. You have a handsome young man to look after you."

My neck still aches, but not as much as when I woke up so I look at Donovan and catch my breath.

The machine lets out weird noises, causing Reece and Donovan to stand straight against the wall.

"Breathe, Mara." She chuckles.

"Which one of you two will be looking after her recovery?"

"That will be me." Donovan moves away from the wall. "She's my girl." He smiles.

"How are you going to look after my sister?"

Reece frowns.

Donovan turns to face him. "Do you have a problem with me looking after my girl?"

"This is weird."

"I want her with me. No, I need her with me." Donovan stands his ground.

"I'm not arguing," Reece states and walks back over to me. "I'm going to go." He kisses me. "You didn't ruin anything—you remember that, okay?"

Nodding hurts, so I grimace, and say, "I will. I love you brother."

"I love you sis. Don't ever frighten me like that again."

"I'll try not too," I whisper.

He pulls Donovan into his arms for a *manly* hug. "Take care of her and get some sleep."

"Yes, Mom."

Chuckling, Reece leaves us in peace.

"I meant it, you know. That I want to look after you—that I want you with me at my place."

"Good, because that's the only place I want to go." My eyes start to droop.

"The nurse snuck some more painkiller into your drip so sleep. I'll be here when you wake up."

"I love you, Donovan."

"I lov—"

I'm asleep before he finishes.

27

DONOVAN

THE BEST THING FOR MY GIRL RIGHT NOW IS TO let her sleep. It's difficult because I just want her awake and smiling at me so I know she's okay.

I've been at the hospital since they brought her in, and by her side since she got out of recovery so I'm exhausted, but unable to leave her.

She looks so fragile sleeping in her bed that it breaks my heart seeing her like this.

Resting my head back down on her bed, I cover her hand with mine and close my eyes. They snap open seconds later when I hear the door open.

"Stay where you are, Donovan," Cindy says moving a chair beside mine as she wraps an arm around my shoulders. "You look ready to drop.

Why don't you go and get some rest while I'm here."

I'm shaking my head before she's even finished speaking. "I won't leave her."

"Let's look at it a different way then. How are you going to look after my daughter when she gets out of here if you're sick yourself?"

Fuck. She has a point. But how the hell can I leave her?

"I'll drive you," Reece offers.

I had no idea that he'd come back into the room. My strength has deserted me. I really don't have the energy to put up much of a struggle.

"Donovan, c'mon man. She's going to need you when she comes home. The last thing she needs is to worry about you as well."

"I hear you." I let out a loud sigh. "Both of you," I add.

"You won't leave her, right?" I ask Cindy.

She offers me a sad smile. "She's my daughter Donovan. I promise not to leave until you get back. Now go and get some proper food inside you and sleep for a bit, and maybe shower."

I burst out laughing.

"Am I that bad?"

"You're getting there. Go. The sooner you get

some food and rest, the sooner you will be back here."

"All right."

My eyes wander back to my girl. Bending close, I kiss her gently on the lips before pulling back. Leaving her is harder than I ever thought.

I mean she isn't in the hospital with a life threatening illness. She has a badly broken arm and swollen ankle, but I love her and I'm worried about her. Her fall frightened the fuck out of me, which I'm not sure I'll ever get out of my head.

Sighing, I give her mom a hug and without looking back because if I do I won't leave, I walk out of the room with Reece—exhausted as fuck.

"DONOVAN, YOU NEED TO WAKE UP."

"Donovan, c'mon man."

I'm going to punch Reece if he doesn't shut up. I've only been asleep for five minutes.

I carry on ignoring him.

"Okay, if you don't wake up I'm going to take a picture of your naked ass with my phone and plaster it all over Facebook . . . 1 . . . 2 . . ."

"Fuck you."

I grab the sheet and pull it over me as I turn to lie on my back. Then it hits me—Mara.

"What time is it," I ask Reece while dashing to the bathroom to relieve myself.

"Three."

Opening the shower door, I quickly step inside and turning the taps on, I catch my breath as the water hits me. *So fuckin' cold!* Well at least it woke me up. If it's three in the afternoon that means I've been out of it for about four hours.

Turning the taps off after what must be the quickest shower in history, I wrap a towel around my hips and walk back into the bedroom to find Reece spread out on my bed.

"If you didn't keep your woman up all night you wouldn't be so tired." I smirk.

"My woman is the one keeping me up. I don't know where the fuck she gets her energy from because I'm fucked."

Laughing at him, I quickly drag clean jeans, tee shirt and boots on before heading out into the front of my house where I stop dead.

How the hell I didn't notice the smell of food while I was in my bedroom is anyone's guess because there is no way this didn't travel. *Chili.* My stomach chooses this moment to grumble.

"Sit. You're not going anywhere until we've fed

you. Cindy rang not five minutes ago to check on you. Mara is more awake now and she's okay. She said to tell you to stop worrying about her and to look after yourself before you go back to the hospital."

With a nod of my head, I acknowledge what Thalia just told me as I sag into the chair at the dinning table.

"Thanks for this girls, and that smells good." My stomach growls again.

"You should have eaten before now," Callie tells me. "She's going to be okay. You know that, right?"

I smile. "Yes, I know she's gong to be fine. And I'll be fine when she's out of that place and back here with me."

"We hear you." Jack sits with me before Reece joins us and then the girls are placing dishes of food on the table—chili, rice and homemade cornbread.

"Dig in," Callie says.

She doesn't need to tell me twice.

Filling my plate with food, I start to eat savoring the flavors. This is damn good and even though I've thanked them, I don't think they realize how much I appreciate this. In fact, until I sat down and started eating, I hadn't realized how hungry I am.

As soon as I climbed in my truck from the hospital, which Reece has been using, I was out for the count waking up briefly to get myself in the house before I stripped and dropped to my bed.

Now, thanks to my friends, I'm refueling and eager to get back to see Mara.

"I'll take you back soon," Reece says. "You were thinking rather loudly," he adds obviously seeing my questioning look for what it was.

"Jack can follow so I have a lift back. That way you can keep your truck with you."

"That will work," I agree.

Taking another piece of cornbread, I scoop up some more chili with it and catch Callie watching me. As I'm shoving it in my mouth, she grins.

Is there something wrong with it?

"You're really enjoying that," Callie states.

"I sure am, and not because I haven't eaten since sometime yesterday. This really is good and you've no idea how much I appreciate you cooking this for me."

"Hey, she's my girl. She cooked it for me."

Callie rolls her eyes. "Reece, just eat and stay out of trouble."

"I thought you liked my kind of trouble."

"I do." She gives him a look, which has his eyes narrowing.

I chuckle.

Pushing my plate away, I stretch and standing up, look to the girls. "Thanks for that."

"You're welcome."

Callie comes and hugs me followed by Thalia. "Take care of yourself."

"I will."

The guys hug and kiss their women before we all trudge outside to the trucks to take me back to the hospital and my girl.

28

MARA

THE PAIN IN MY ARM IS MANAGEABLE AT THE moment so while I can handle it I'm refusing anything stronger because I don't want to be out of it when Donovan gets back here.

I've eaten all my lunch because I was so hungry, and I'm not sure why people complain about hospital food because that wasn't too bad. I'm just glad my mom has finally gone for a walk to the shop to get me something fizzy and some chocolate. My sweet tooth is calling.

I'm trying to concentrate on the magazine that Mom brought me, but I'm just not in the mood and I feel restless. I know what I'm restless for and that is for Donovan to get back here. I know he needed some rest and proper food, but I just want him here.

I'm really trying not to be too clingy with him, but I feel as though something is missing when we're not together.

Looking toward the opening door to my room, my heart flutters hoping it's Donovan then drops to my toes when I see Sarah.

"Can I come in?"

"I guess."

Sarah looks nervous as she approaches my bed with her hands flexing around the straps of her purse.

She sits in the chair beside me.

"How are you feeling?"

Does she really care?

I answer her anyway, "Not too bad."

"Good. Good."

We sit in silence for a few minutes. I can't help hoping that Mom will get back soon to save me and I've no idea what Sarah's thinking about.

Finally having enough of the silence, I ask, "Why are you here?"

She flinches as though I've hit her and I watch as her eyes tear up. "I'm sorry, Mara." She swipes at a wayward tear. "I've been a bitch to you and I'm sorry. I'm sorry for calling you a whore. I'm just damn sorry about everything. I'm pissed, okay. So damn angry—not at you—at someone else or me. I haven't decided properly. Anyway, the truth is I do like Donovan but not in the way you obviously do. Okay, perhaps that's a lie. I used to like Donovan that way, but I haven't for a long while. He just seemed handy to get my own back on someone. No matter though, you're my sister and I shouldn't have treated you that way. I'm sorry."

I'm stunned. I never in a million years expected her to apologize to me. And who is this someone she's referring to? She's so damn private. I need to accept her apology though if we're going to move forward. She's my sister after all.

"Apology accepted. Who are you talking about?"

"It doesn't matter."

"Yes it does. If they caused you to act like you have been then it matters."

"It's just some guy I met at college. We dated a few times, well more like three months and then it went to shit. I'm good now and I really am sorry for being a bitch with you and Donovan."

"Okay, but what about Dahlia? Why did you blackmail her?"

"Oh God," she puts her head in her hands. "That was so stupid. Part of me stills blames her for Dad, even though I know it isn't her fault which just doesn't make any sense. When I saw what I did, I thought it would keep her away from us and it didn't work in the end. I just can't accept her yet. I'm not ready and I'm not sure if I ever will be. I don't want to talk any more about that."

"Okay."

"I better go." She kisses me on the forehead and then chuckles when she sees my stunned expression. "I wish I had my phone handy to capture that look."

"I'm surprised."

"That's sad really because you shouldn't be surprised. But we'll work on it."

"Okay."

On her way over to the door, it starts to open and this time my heart beats so damn fast when I see my sexy man walking in. He's changed clothes and shaved, making him look a lot better than he did when he left here hours before.

He checks me out. "Are you okay?"

"I'm fine."

"Donovan, I want to apologize." Sarah steps in front of him. "I'm not going to get into it, but I'm sorry for being a bitch. You won't have to worry about me from now on. I'm going to try and get back to being sisters with Mara instead of enemies."

"That's good."

"I'm going. Take care of my sister for me."

And with that, she's gone.

"Um. Seriously?"

I grin. "Yep. Hopefully it will last longer than a week."

Donovan shakes his head and comes over to me. He rests his arm on my pillow and caresses my face. "I missed you."

"I missed you too, but I'm glad you went and got some rest. You looked shattered." I take hold of his hand with mine and kiss his palm.

He kisses my nose before sitting in the chair he's spent a lot of time in.

"Thalia and Callie made some chili and corn-bread." He grins. "It was really good."

"I bet it was. I'm glad they're taking care of you while I'm stuck in here," I say, my voice husky with tears.

Donovan scoots closer and rests his chin on our joined hands. "You're coming home tomorrow to my house. I wish you were coming to live with me under different circumstances, but I can't wait to have you there. In my bed with my arms around you while you sleep."

"I'm really going to cry." I sniff. "Can you pass me a tissue?"

Getting back to his feet, he grabs a handful of tissues and uses them to mop me up. "You can cry any time you want and I'll always be here to dry them."

I groan. "I love hearing those words, but can you wait until I'm not so emotional. My face will be all blotchy like it probably is now."

He starts to laugh. How can he laugh at me when I'm in the hospital crying?

"Now babe. Stop frowning at me. You look damn cute."

He kisses my frowning lips with his smiling ones.

"I love you," he whispers.

And that does it. How can I be mad at him when he tells me I look cute even though I know I'm blotchy and when he can say "I love you" when I'm not at my best.

29

DONOVAN

"Reece, you are seriously pissing me off," Mara shouts to her brother's back as he leaves my place.

She's been living here with me for two days now and is getting frustrated as hell not being able to get around on her sprained ankle. The trip downstairs took place four days ago and no matter what anyone tells her, she thinks her ankle should be back to a hundred percent by now. Part of me is relieved that Reece came around when he did because he got the brunt of her temper.

I suppose I'd be pissed as well, not able to get about and being cooped up indoors, but that's about to change. While she was chatting to her brother, I've set up the new sun lounger that he brought around for me. She loves the hammock, but until her ankle is better this is the next best thing. It's even better because it's one of the double ones so I can cuddle up with my girl and hopefully calm her down.

Entering the bedroom, I lean against the doorframe and watch her fight back tears, probably tears of frustration.

"Hey babe." Gently climbing on the bed beside her, I lean over her and kiss her lips, her forehead, her nose and back to her lips. "I have a surprise for you?"

"You're going to make love to me."

I groan.

"When you can move"

"I can move now." She wraps her arms around my neck.

"Without being in pain."

"Spoil sport," she pouts.

Laughing, I pull away from her. "C'mon. I want to show you your surprise. Grab your kindle."

I pull the throw from the bottom of the bed that she's partial to and then scoop her up in my arms. "Hold tight, baby."

I carry her through my home, which I hope one day she'll call her own. This is the only place I can imagine living with her, although if the truth be told, I'd live anywhere she wanted to just to be with her. She's my home now. I just don't want to scare the shit out of her with her being younger than me.

"Oh wow. You did this for me?" She covers her mouth with her hands as tears form in her eyes.

"I'd do anything for you, babe. Let's check it out." I place her down gently on her side and get the cushion in the right place behind her head before covering her up with the blanket. Once I'm sure she's settled, I lie down beside her and take her hand in mine. We are silent as we gaze out at the view of the lake.

"So this is what all the noise was while Reece was inside annoying me?"

"It was and what did Reece do?"

"He wanted to know what was going to happen between us when we both went back to the city."

A question I'd been dreading because I wasn't all that sure I wanted to go back and was planning on talking to her to see whether she wanted to stay in the city or transfer back here. Part of me feels selfish though. How can I ask her to do that? She is happy with her new program of study and to have her work displayed in an art show in the museum was amazing. It was also something that wouldn't have happened back here.

"Why are you so quiet?"

"Thinking."

She laughs. "Well, scoot over here and wrap me in your arms. I need you close."

Well hell.

The things this girl does to my heart is crazy.

Rubbing my chest, I turn on my side and carefully bring her into me. She snuggles back against my chest as I spoon around her.

The bruises she collected during her tumble are still there although not as vivid as they were and she's certainly moving a lot easier than she was. Her ankle and arm still cause her pain, which is why I have a stock of Tylenol because she refuses the prescribed painkillers. When I have her in my arms like she is now, I never want to move. There is nothing more satisfying than having the girl I love close to my heart.

"Donovan, you're thinking so loud that I can hear you."

Smiling, I kiss her on the back of her neck. "I was thinking how lucky I am to have you—how much I love you—how much I love having you living with me and how much I love you, as well as what Reece wanted to know. We need to talk about it because I'm not sure I want you away from me. Before we were living together, I hated you leaving, and now I want to be selfish and hold you close." I bury my face into the back of her neck and breathe her scent in to my lungs.

"I'm not sure what you're thinking, but if you think you're going to be able to get rid of me now I'm here, you can think again. I'm here to stay."

I can hear the smile in her voice.

"That's settled then. You're living with me from now on."

Mara wiggles and lying on her back, she kicks the blanket off with her good leg as I move and lean over her, so desperate to take her mouth with mine. But I'm afraid I won't be able to stop and end up hurting her. Even now just having her eyes on me, my dick is hard as fuck and tenting my sweats. I knew there was a reason why I needed to wear shorts beneath. There's no way she won't feel what she's doing to me, and catching her wandering hand in mine, I catch the laughter on her face.

Using my other hand, I shove the waistband of my sweats over the tip of my cock to keep it against my stomach instead of prodding against her.

Mara gasps then moans. "Please let me touch you."

I have a happy dick hearing those words, but no way in hell.

"Keep your hands to yourself babe. The next time you touch me will be *after* I've shown you what it's like to be loved." I place a quick kiss to her lips before rolling onto my back.

"I'm really frustrated," she grumbles.

"You're not the only one." I close my eyes to try and catch my breath.

"What will it feel like when you slide inside me?"

Is she trying to kill me?

"Donovan?"

"What?"

"You didn't answer," she smirks.

Keeping my eyes shut, I grind out, "Heaven. Being inside your tight wet pussy will be heaven."

Talking about her pussy and my dick isn't helping my *horny* problem so with that in mind, I ask, "What about school? What do you want to do?"

"Hmm. I know you're changing the subject, but I'll let you off for now." She rolls on to her good side and rests her injured arm on my chest as she uses my shoulder for a cushion. "I want to carry on studying art, but where I do that doesn't matter to me. All that matters is if you're with me. If you want to stay in the city we can do that or if you want to stay here then I can transfer back. The college when I left said if I changed my mind about city living to come see them so that sounds good right? But what do you want to do?"

"I'm going to go back to college and do what I've wanted to do for years. So babe, I'm going to let you choose because I'll most certainly follow. I'll always follow you." And I mean every word. I just hope she realizes that.

"If we go back to the city, where will I be living?" She starts to draw circles with her fingernail on my chest.

"With me! Where else do you think you'll be living?"

"That makes me happy."

Brushing the hair back from her neck, I start a gentle caress. "Mara, are you sure this is what you want? That I'm what you want?"

She stills against me.

"Donovan—"

"You're eighteen Mara. You have your whole life ahead of you. I love you too much to let you tie yourself down now with me if you're unsure."

Burying her face in my chest, she stays silent, but a few seconds later I feel dampness against me.

"I'm in love with you. I don't think you can get more certain than that. Besides you're not exactly an old man." She sniffles.

"That's all I wanted to know. And for the

record if you'd responded differently I think you'd have killed me."

"Then let's live here. I will talk to my old advisor at the college and I know they do have architectural design courses. That is what you want right?"

"Yes, that's what I want. I also miss this place when I'm away so it will be good to move back. We'll have to work something out with Deception because I won't be around much."

She groans. "I'd forgotten about them. I'm sorry."

"Don't be sorry. This is a move I've wanted to make for a while and if you hadn't moved to the city when you did then I'd have already been back."

She looks up to me and meets my eyes. "I don't understand."

"When I was looking for a place to stay it was my way of building up the courage to tell the guys I wanted to move back home. I wanted to see if the feelings I have for you were real. But all I had to do was open the door to see you breaking your heart to know that they are. So I got another apartment close by and then proceeded to ignore you because I'm an idiot. So basically, I don't give a shit where I live as long you're with me."

"I can't stop crying."

Rubbing her back, I try and console her and pull her closer to me just needing that extra bit of contact. But then I get too much contact when she slides her leg in between mine and bringing her knee up slightly, she rubs against my balls causing my dick to twitch and take notice.

"Donovan," she whispers just before she bites my nipple causing me to arch into her.

"We can't do this." My hands slide on to her bottom and squeeze, pressing her against me. "We really can't do this." She captures my mouth with hers and as soon as our tongues meet, I'm lost. She removes her leg from between mine and swings it over my hip bringing her pussy against my dick nearly making my eyes roll back in my head.

"I ache," she moans into my mouth as she rubs against me.

Breathing heavily, I break completely from the kiss and rest my forehead against hers. "Let me re-lieve you?"

"What about you?" She gasps when I press forward with my hips.

"I'll survive."

"Ahhh, fuck, baby," I hiss when her hand slips between our bodies and squeezes my length.

If I don't stop this I'm going to be giving her more than she bargained for by coming all over us.

Grabbing hold of her leg, I help her get comfortable before stripping her shorts and panties down her legs and tossing them to the floor.

"You are beautiful," I kneel between her spread thighs, "so beautiful." Reaching out, I stroke the top of her pussy where she has a landing strip and feel a ripple of pleasure working it's way through her. When I dip further between her legs, she gasps and then moans, her hips slightly arching toward me.

"I'm going to taste you," her eyes darken at my words, "but only if you promise not to move. I want to pleasure you not hurt you."

"I promise. Just do it."

I chuckle. "Impatient little thing, aren't you?"

She doesn't reply but groans when my finger slips inside her. She's so tight and her muscles clamping around just the tip of my digit are causing my dick to swell and leak with excitement.

"Wait," she gasps. "Strip."

"What?"

"Help me," she pleads, struggling with her clothes.

I toss her tee shirt followed by her bra to the floor and watch as she stares back at me. I have to close my eyes from the sight of her excited nipples beading under my gaze, which she notices and brings her hands up to cover them before she starts rubbing over them with her fingers. My dick surges against my sweats knowing what it fuckin' wants.

Before she can blink, I have my tee shirt off and my sweats around my thighs and then her hand lands on my straining length. I nearly lose it as my hips arch in to her touch.

She caresses back and forth, wiping the head with her thumb. I grind my molars while trying to stay loaded because she's making me want to come all over her generous breasts. I'm sure it's every man's fantasy or dirty dream to fuck his girl's boobs. To play with her nipples while squeezing her breasts around his shaft as he rocks between the luscious softness that only he has access to.

Fuck!

I knock her hand away and breathing heavily through my nose desperate to come, I press down on my balls. This is supposed to be about my girl, but somehow we've gone off track.

Hoping I manage to keep it together long enough to pleasure her, I lie down between her legs. "Be careful with your foot and just keep your arm resting against the lounger."

"Hmm."

Smiling, I dip down and catch her scent before using my tongue to part her silken folds.

I growl.

"You taste good."

Pointing my tongue, I glide between her pussy lips, aiming for her most secret depths. It makes me feel so damn excited knowing she's letting me go where no one else has been before. Knowing my cock is going to be buried in her tight heat as soon as she's back on her feet is making me burn up. I've never been with a virgin before, and knowing it's the girl that I'm in love with does weird things inside me.

Swirling my tongue around her entrance, I finally get a taste of her essence and my balls pull in tight to my body. *So not good.* But I can't slow down.

She writhes under my onslaught. Feeling so close to my own release, I insert my finger as my tongue laves her clit and start to massage along her walls. Feeling her legs quiver and small gasps escape her mouth, I rub against the bundle of nerves and take all of her release in my mouth as hot spurts of cum shoot out of dick in my own release.

30

MARA

When Donovan carried me out back and laid me down on here, I hadn't planned for us to get carried away. Poor, Donovan though, he'd planned the perfect romantic evening for us for after my brother's wedding and I ended up nearly killing myself. Just my luck.

Once I'm back on my feet I'm going to make it up to him, but right now having the man I'm in love with resting his face on my pussy is turning me on again—so much. I'm exhausted from the orgasm he's just given me, but my body wants more. I have a feeling my heart and body will always want more of him. He treats me like a princess, which will change, but while I'm laid up I'm willing to sit back, or rather lie back and let him.

I need to finish him off though—I'm not selfish. He must be in pain suppressing his need. So with that in mind, I use my good arm and try to pull him up my body, but he doesn't budge. "Donovan. I need you up here."

He lifts his head and slowly crawls up me, kissing each breast. "These are beautiful."

"They're too big."

"Like hell. They're just the right size. One day I'm going to fuck your breasts."

My eyes widen in shock. I know I'm a virgin and read erotica genre in books, but hearing Donovan come out with something surprises me. I have wondered about it after reading it, and the thought makes me want to tell him to get his dick up here and to straddle my chest. He's so dirty and I'm getting frustrated as hell that he won't make love to me. I understand why, and I understand that he wants to make it special for me. But doesn't he understand that just being with him—that he's the guy—is special. There are a lot of things I want to try out and one of them is to be taken up against a wall in public. I don't mean with an audience, but where there is a risk of us being caught. It sounds hot and gets me excited every time I think about it.

"What are you thinking about? You're eyes have

darkened with lust again and your hips are moving with a mind of their own."

"I'm thinking that my guy is dirty and that I want to get down and dirty with him. But you need to deflower me first because I'm getting desperate to have you inside me. I've seen and touched you, and know how big you are and I clench wanting you sliding in and out of me."

"Fuck me, Mara," he growls. "We need to get dressed before the guys and girls get here.

"We're having visitors?"

"Yeah. You've looked down all day so I thought they could come round for a bit." He smiles. "They're bringing beer and pizza."

"Okay." I stroke a finger down the center of his chest. "But I still want you up here. I want your full weight on me when you hold me close."

"Oh baby." He moves from my aching nipples and comes closer, but we both gasp when I wrap my legs around his hips and the head of his shaft touches me right where I need him. And by the feel of things he's hard and ready again. "Don't move," he grounds out.

"I need to and you need to come."

He presses his dick down so it's lying from my pussy to ass between my legs as he gives me his weight.

"I came at the same time you did."

"You did?" I seriously hadn't realized.

"Yeah. I'll flip the cover and then wash it later."

"Um, okay."

I wrap my arms around his shoulders, taking care not to bash him with the one in the plaster, and hold him tight. He buries his face in my neck.

He feels so good against me and having his dick between my legs is hot especially when it twitches. Its light caress is making me want to flip him over and slide down on him. But I'm not going to do that because not only will it hurt, it will disappoint him. He wants to be romantic for my first time so I'll have to control my body's urges, which is easier said than done. I want to stay wrapped around him like this forever, but unfortunately my ankle is starting to throb and we have guests arriving soon.

Dropping my legs back to the lounger, I wince when my sore ankle hits. *Bad idea.*

Donovan lifts his head. "You need some more painkillers, babe. Let me carry you inside and clean you up before putting fresh clothes on."

"Okay. I kind of like having you doing things for me, although I have a feeling it's going to get pretty old fast."

He chuckles, then places a kiss to my lips before

sorting himself out and carrying me inside to the bathroom where he seats me on the vanity unit.

Wetting a cloth he turns and grins at me. "Open wide," he says, wiggling his brows. "Mara. Now isn't the time to be stubborn. I want to look after you."

Rolling my eyes, I spread my thighs and smile when I catch sight of his cock swelling.

"Stop looking at me, Mara, or I won't be responsible for the consequences." He wipes between my legs—thoroughly.

Without another word he carries me back into the bedroom and sitting me on the side of the bed grabs me fresh underwear, yoga pants and a tee shirt before helping me dress. My body comes alive under his touch so I tease, "You know, I think there's something wrong with me?"

"Why'd you say that?"

"Because up until two weeks ago my body was kind of flat you know, but since we've been back here and I've been with you, my body is constantly wanting to have sex with you. That can't be normal for a virgin."

He groans with his cock twitching.

"Don't move."

He dashes into the bathroom and I hear the

shower switch on, and then a crash followed by some cussing.

"Are you okay?"

"I'm fine. Give me a minute."

Collapsing back on the bed, I gaze up at the ceiling wishing I could join him in the shower. Once I no longer have my *flower,* I'm going to seduce him every damn opportunity I get. He's going to wonder what the hell is wrong with me having a horny girlfriend 24/7 because that's how I feel—constantly horny. I wonder if he reacts like that to me.

Speaking of the devil, he comes out of the bathroom with a towel wrapped around his waist and, ignoring me, he grabs shorts, jeans and a tee shirt. Pulling his clothes on he drops on his stomach to the bed beside me.

"To answer your question, now I'm dressed, the answer is your *horny* feelings toward me are perfectly normal," he laughs as I lightly punch him on the arm. "Seriously babe. You love me right so is natural you'd want me all the time. I mean I love you and can't get you out of my head. For a while now, I only have to hear your voice down the phone and I'm hard as a rock. One touch from you is enough to have me nearly coming in my jeans. I mean outside, you didn't even touch me and I came when you did."

God, I love his smile, and his sexy body and I just plain love him.

He rubs noses with me. "So does that answer your question?"

"It answers my question but it doesn't do anything about the craving to constantly have sex with you. In fact, just to have sex once with you would be good," I grumble.

He laughs. "We've done some pretty hot stuff babe and I promise I'm going to be inside you really soon."

"But not soon enough."

He groans and drops his face in to the bed.

"Anyone home?" Thalia shouts.

"Yeah. One minute," Donovan replies getting to his feet and readjusting himself in his jeans.

"C'mon babe. Let's go eat and be social for a short while."

He's in the process of picking me up in his arms when I remember, "Our clothes are still out back," wrapping my arms around his neck.

"Fuck."

Carrying me out into the family room, he deposits me into the recliner. "I'll hide them." He kisses me on the lips and moves away.

"I hope you brought plenty of pizza. Mara's hungry."

"Very funny." I'm not that hungry, but Donovan can eat and I mean really eat.

"How you doing today?" Thalia asks sitting opposite while Callie sits to my right.

"Frustrated."

They look at me before looking back and forth between the two of them when I start laughing.

"Well, I am that, but I meant not being able to get around myself. It's starting to piss me off. Donovan's great, and although I love being in his arms, it's frustrating that he has to take me to the bathroom, you know?"

"He loves you and won't give a damn about all that."

"I know. Anyway, enough about me when are you both going away seems as though I ruined your original plans?"

"Oh, you hush now. You didn't ruin anything," Thalia tells me the same thing they've been saying since my fall. I still feel bad though. She continues, "We're going to the beach tomorrow for a couple of days."

"Nice. Hopefully my brother will come back in a better mood."

"He's just worried about you," Callie says.

"I know. He just goes overboard with it sometimes."

"Hey sis. Feeling better?" Reece kisses me on the head before grabbing Callie up out of the chair. "Let's go outside now Donovan's tided up."

I look everywhere but at him when he said that. Tided up my ass. More like hidden our clothes and any sign of us fooling around.

"Hmm. Now what would make you embarrassed about going outside," Thalia smirks.

"Just don't tell my brother."

"Don't tell your brother what?" Donovan asks having overheard me.

"Why I'm blushing because you've tided up outside."

Donovan pauses as he's in the process of bending down to collect me and meets my gaze, and then he grins like a satisfied idiot.

"Nothing to be embarrassed about," he says, kissing me now that I'm in his arms.

He strides outside and sits me down at the table where there are four, huge pizza boxes and two, six packs of beer and some Pepsi spread out.

My stomach chooses this moment to grumble —loudly.

They laugh, and Reece asks Donovan, "You not feeding my sister, man?"

"I'm feeding her just fine."

The guys open the boxes and the fresh pizza smell hits me again. "Did you get these from the new place in town?" I ask taking a huge bite from the slice of cheese and mushroom pizza Donovan placed on my plate.

"Sure did and it isn't new anymore. It's been there over twelve months," Jack adds.

"Exactly, it's still new." I grin. "Before I left to join y'all in the city, I'd go there and sit in the kitchen with Marco. While he'd get the dough ready and all the fresh ingredients for the food, I'd keep him company. Sometimes I'd help, but mostly I'd just sit and inhale the delicious aromas."

I carry on eating and notice Donovan looking at me, so I return his gaze, raising an eyebrow in question.

"Marco?" he asks.

Reece chuckles. "A bit of jealousy never did anyone any harm."

Donovan grunts. "I'm still waiting."

"He's a really good looking guy, and he likes me. He used to save me some of his tiramisu if I didn't show up the day he'd made it." Now I laugh. There is no way I can carry on pretending. "Marco also has a great grandchild that I'd look after sometimes when his mom was cleaning in the restaurant.

Marco is eighty-six with no sign of giving up his kitchen."

"She got you there," Jack says with a punch to Donovan's arm.

Donovan wraps his fingers around mine, which are sticking out of the plaster cast that I have resting in my lap. I find it cumbersome, but having him touching me while we're here with my brother, Jack and their wives is amazing. I never thought I'd have this with him.

31

DONOVAN

"You better not be doing what I think you're doing with your hand on my sister's, um, there?" Reece stumbles over his words causing the others to erupt with laughter.

"Are you for real?" Mara asks, but I don't think she's expecting an answer.

"You're an idiot. As though I'd be feeling her up with you sitting there." I shake my head. "I want to hold my girl's hand if that's okay with you?"

Reece opens his mouth and I watch as Callie shoves a slice of pizza in. "You need to keep your mouth occupied with something other than words before you say something to piss them off."

"Hey. I'm cool with them being together."

Callie snorts—very unladylike.

Mara stills next to me.

"You really are okay with me being with Donovan, right? I mean, reverse psyche shit and all that."

"Of course I—"

He rubs his arm that Callie pinched.

"I think I'm going to need insurance being married to you. I was about to say before I was so rudely interrupted that of course I'm okay with you both being together." He grins.

"What a load of shit." Callie bursts out laughing.

God, he's giving me a headache. He told me reverse psychology, so what the fuck is going on.

"Okay, to begin with I was pissed, but then as time went on I realized it was more so I decided the reverse psychology crap," he smiles, "and it worked. Although on occasion I had second thoughts."

"Ha, yeah right." Callie smirks at Reece before looking at Mara. "You should have heard him the night of the art show. He wasn't okay then."

"Wife, eat some pizza," Reece says before he adds, "I'm okay with you both being together. Now can we please change the topic of conversation?" He takes a large bite from his fully loaded slice.

Mara squeezes my fingers so I turn to look at her and see a small smile on her lips. She leans into me and I meet her halfway placing a small kiss to her lips. "Are you doing okay?" I whisper, sliding my hand into her glorious hair.

"I'm always all right when I'm with you." She grins.

"Okay, enough of that mushy shit with my sister. Let's go down to the lake and leave the girls here to gossip." Reece stands up, kisses Callie like he's leaving for a month before grabbing another beer.

Jack kisses Thalia and starts to follow Reece with his beer so that leaves me with three pairs of female eyes on me.

Laughing, Mara wraps her good arm around my neck and pulls me close for one, hot kiss that has my toes curling and my dick swelling. Pulling back she grins at me with lust clear as day on her face. But unfortunately we can't do anything about that right now.

"I'll see you soon babe." I push away from the table and, grabbing a beer, turn back to Mara, "You'll be okay, right?"

"I'll be fine. Don't worry. It's not as though you're too far away. One shout and you'll be here."

"Okay." I quickly kiss her again. "See you girls real soon."

Shoving my feet into my sneakers, I walk away from my house, and listen to the girls laughing.

Probably at my expense, but I really don't care. Mara has me wrapped around her little finger and I love her. I love her taste, which is addictive and causes my blood to heat with arousal. I love her sense of humor and her laughter. I love the way she thinks and all of her passion for art. Let's face it, I love all of her.

Arriving at the small jetty where my dad's boat is moored, I'm tempted to turn back to my girl, but the grinning faces of my two idiotic friends stop me.

"You are so easy to read," Jack shouts, laughing. "She isn't going to disappear."

"Whatever."

Kicking my sneakers off, I drop down and let the cool water of the lake lap around my feet and ankles. Jack and Reece join me.

"Come with us," Reece says out of the blue and I've no idea what he's talking about.

"What?"

"You heard me. Come with us when we take the girls to the beach tomorrow."

I look between my two best friends to gauge whether or not they're serious about Mara and me joining them, and they look to be.

"Why would you want me to tag along on your honeymoon? I don't think Mara would like me helping you guys out pleasuring your girls," I smirk when I see the shocked expressions on their faces.

I'm not serious, but I love winding them up, and no doubt they'll get me back at some point.

Jack hits me in the arm. "My girl is plenty satisfied so shut the fuck up."

"I'm not even going to dignify that with an answer," Reece growls.

Smiling, I take a drink of my beer then grimace because the beer has warmed up with the heat. We usually put them in coolers, but I had my girl in my arms and my head so the coolers slipped my mind. Not sure what my friends excuses are.

Taking another drag on the bottle, I rest back on my elbows and look up at the moon trying to think whether or not I want to head to the beach with my girl and the guys. Do I want to keep her to myself or share her is what it basically comes down to.

"Well? You coming with us?" Reece persists.

"I'm thinking."

"Well think faster."

"Why the rush? It's not as though you're going now."

"I like to plan."

"Yeah right." I turn to Jack. "What about you? Are you really okay if Mara and me come with you?"

"I've just shared a wedding with one of my best friends so why wouldn't I want my other best friend to come on honeymoon with me?" He grins wiggling his eyebrows.

"You're both dicks," I laugh. "We'll go with you, but we're not having separate rooms. Non negotiable."

"Well, we sure as hell aren't sharing a room with your hairy ass," Jack jokes, laughing.

"Ha ha. Funny man!"

"Perhaps this isn't such a good idea," Reece frowns. "I'm not sure I can cope with you sharing a room with my sister."

"Are you for real? We're already sharing a house. Dick!"

"He has a point," Jack comments. "She might be your sister, but she's his girl so quit being so damn protective of her when you know he wouldn't hurt her for anything."

"I knew there was a reason why I loved you." I grin wrapping my arm around Jack's neck.

"Um, is there something you need to tell us?" Thalia asks.

How the hell they managed to creep up behind us, I don't know. The damn jetty creeks like the bones on a ninety-year old man—my grandfather's description, not mine.

Turning, I see Mara being held up between Callie and Thalia. Jumping to my feet, I wrap my arms around her waist. She releases her hold on the girls and wraps her arms around my neck just missing knocking me out with the arm in the plaster cast. That's more inconvenient than the ankle.

"What are you doing struggling down here?"

"We finished eating and I wanted to be with you." She looks uncertain. "I mean you don't mind, right? Or do you?"

She starts removing her arms from around me, which won't do and I'm being an idiot for not reply- ing. It's just that hearing that she has struggled down here between the girls because she wants to be with me fills me with joy, but at the same time I don't want her hurting because of me.

Tightening my hold on her, I bend my head and kiss her sweet spot on her neck, which always makes her shiver. And she does again. "I love that you want to be with me, and don't think for one minute that I'm mad with you for interrupting when I'm with the guys. They're my best friends and probably always will be, but you're the girl I love and you will always come first. You got me?"

She nods her head and probably hoping I don't notice, buries her tear stained face in my neck. I do all I can to comfort her and carry on holding her close, when Reece has to go and interrupt.

"So you're telling me that we don't come first anymore?"

Turning, but keeping my hands on Mara, I reply, "That's about right." I grin.

Reece tries to hold his frown, but it slips and ends up a shit-eating grin.

"I promise to try and stop being a dick where my sister is concerned, but you ever hurt her then all bets are off."

"I hear you."

I've no intention of ever hurting my girl. We're bound to have arguments now and again, but I can't ever imagine doing something to hurt her. There is one thing that I'm going to be doing, which will probably hurt the guys though so I decide now while it's quiet to tell them about the changes I'm making to my life.

"Let's sit back down, I need to tell you all something."

Through the dark, I feel them watching me as they do what I ask.

I help Mara get to the floor before I sit behind her and pull her back against my chest to wrap my arms around her stomach.

"Mara and I have been talking about living

arrangements and college." Now or never. "We've decided to live here, as in this house and Mara is going to finish her studying here and I'm going back to concentrate on architectural design."

No one says anything, and then they all start talking at once.

I wait for them to shut up rather than trying to talk over them. I might as well save my breath.

Mara leans against my shoulder and I meet her amused gaze. My eyes drop to her lips and all the noise disappears. All I can hear is the blood rushing through my ears and all I can see is the beautiful girl in my arms. I capture her lips and nothing else matters. Her mouth opens for more so slipping my tongue inside, I stroke against hers. Until we hear a throat being cleared, which is when I realize the noise has stopped.

Separating, we grin at each other before facing everyone.

"At least I can think now. I told Mara that I'd be willing to stay in the city if that is what she wanted. In fact, I told her I'd go anywhere she wanted. But as it happens she wants to come back here." I caress Mara's face as she looks up at me with love in her eyes before continuing, "I'm more than happy to stay here with Mara. The house is great for us and much better than the apartments in the city. You guys know how much I love to draw, and I've always wanted to do something with that." This is harder than I thought. "So now I'm finally going to do something about it. The only problem I see is Deception. I don't want to leave you guys, but I'm not sure what else we can do." There it's all out in the open.

Reece and Jack grin at me as their wives start laughing.

Mara looks to me, but I've no clue as to what's going on. I expected frowns not grins.

"What's the joke?" I finally ask.

"We were trying to work out a way of telling you that we planned on moving back here once the girls finished college next month. We just hadn't gotten around to it."

"Chickened out, more like," Thalia smirks.

"Whatever. It's a damn relief knowing we're all going to be back here," Reece comments.

Jack kisses his girl and adds, "It sure is."

I drop my face into Mara's neck with a sigh of relief.

32

MARA

I'm feeling much better now that we've spent two days at the beach. Not only has being away cheered me up, but it feels amazing being part of a group. The guys I've known since I could walk but the girls are great as well. For the first time in my life I feel like I'm part of something. I know I'm part of a large family, but this is different. My mom treats Donovan like a son, and has done so since he lost his parents and my sisters have accepted him as my boyfriend. Even Sarah has been on her best behavior and visited me at Donovan's house.

Speaking of Donovan, he is frustrating the hell out of me. After our afternoon on the lounger, he hasn't touched me in a sexual way. I know he wants me because I go to sleep with his swollen dick resting against my bottom, and when I wake up he's just as hard.

Well, if he thinks I'm going to go one more night as a virgin he can think again. Which is why I'm standing in the bathroom checking out my tan line of all things against the lemon colored lacy panties I'm wearing. And apart from them, I'm in matching *fuck-me* shoes and nothing else. My ankle isn't as strong as it was, but I think I can manage from here to the bed. I will even if it kills me. I didn't have the contraception injection to not have sex. Now all I have to do is work up the courage to go out there because for some reason I'm a bag of nerves. Being nervous because I'm about to seduce the man I love is pissing me off. It's not as though I'm totally innocent with the dirty things we've done but I've never had to seduce him before. So, yeah, I'm nervous.

Inhaling, I slowly exhale as I open the bathroom door. I slowly start to walk toward the bed where Donovan is lounging, but leaning over the side table fiddling with his iPhone charger.

Finishing up, he turns to face me and I'm delighted to watch his eyes bulge with shock. "What, um," he laughs, "I give up. Speech is highly overrated."

Meeting me at the end of the bed, he doesn't yet touch me. He gazes into my eyes and lets me see all the love he has for me in his. I only hope he can see everything I feel for him in mine.

Taking that last step into him, my nipples rub against his already naked chest sending a ripple of pleasure down my spine. He gives me a wry smile as I ask, "Please will you make love to me? It's time I felt the slide of your penis inside me." I grin, watching the intense look that crosses his face as he's trying to rein in his control.

"Say something."

He takes my hand and places it over the hard bulge in his shorts. "I want you so much that I'm frightened I'm not going to be able to make it good for you before I release." He removes my hand.

"We have all night."

I kneel on the bed and crawl—the best I can with one arm in plaster—up to the top. Hearing a growl, I know Donovan's watching my bottom.

Staying on my hands and knees, I turn my head and, yeah, he's eyeing my butt. Giving it a wiggle, I ask, "You planning on joining me anytime soon?"

He doesn't need telling twice and drops his shorts to the floor. I grin at the sight. He's sporting an enormous erection. *Will he fit?* Runs through my mind and not for the first time. He twitches and jerks.

"Mara," he bites out, "will you stop looking at me there?"

"You're big," I blurt out.

He laughs. "I aim to please. Now don't move."

He crawls on the bed behind me and bites me on the bottom, his hands going to my hips as he changes sides with his mouth. Within seconds, I'm feeling his hard shaft pressing against me. I push back into him and he growls.

"I need your skin," he impatiently says then my panties are ripped from me. "That's better," he says, and then hisses when his cock rests against my buttocks. I wiggle. He grips my hips for dear life.

"You feel too good." Moving back from me he turns me over so my back is flat on the bed and spreads my legs before crawling between.

"My shoes."

"Leave them on. They're sexy."

He kisses me on my inner thigh—my legs quiver.

"Are you sure you're ready?" he asks, his voice husky.

"I've been ready since the moment you first kissed me."

He pauses mid kisses, smiles and carries on.

Gentle kisses up and down my thighs are causing my pussy to clench with excitement, but he always misses touching where I want him the most. The smirk on his face tells me he knows exactly what he's doing to me.

"Slow baby. By the time I enter you, I want you ready to come apart surrounding me. Because I'm sure as hell going to detonate the minute I'm engulfed in your tight, wet heat."

And at last he dips his head and lets his tongue work it's magic causing my nipples to peak and my back to arch from the bed. He's so good with his mouth and tongue. Lapping at my pussy with his tongue as though he's never tasted me before. My hand reaches for his head and my fingers thread into his hair and hold him against me. I wish I had full use of both of my hands and that I could reach more of him.

His shoulders are so wide and he has the body of a Greek god. All bronzed from the sun, muscles from the gym and lugging all the heavy equipment around when Deception has a show or at the bar where he worked. But right now, watching him between my legs is so damn hot.

"Oh God," I moan. His fingers are now assisting his tongue. I'm not going to last. My hand clenches in the covers, which I find frustrating because I can't anchor my other side due to the cast, but oh God. My orgasm is building. The blood rushes through my ears, my heart is pounding and the man between my legs isn't for giving up. He's pushing me higher and then, "Oh God. Donovan."

"Let go."

My climax hits. I shudder and thrash around under his talented mouth, but before I come back down to earth, he's looming over me. The head of his dick pushing against the entrance no one has been before. I should be nervous, but all I want is to feel him. Just him, and I'm so glad that we don't need to use anything.

33

DONOVAN

I'M GOING TO BE LUCKY IF I DON'T RELEASE right here, right now. She has me by the balls. Having her coming on my tongue caused me to leak uncontrollably and one touch on my cock would have sent me to heaven. But the only heaven I want right now is to be buried deep inside her before I let go.

While she's still in the thralls of orgasm, I rear up and leaning over her, I rest on my arms at either side of her shoulders while the head of my dick nudges against her opening lips. I've never been as desperate to get inside anyone before, as I am Mara.

Keeping my balance with one arm, I reach down and wrapping my hand around my shaft, I rub against her before I slowly start to slide inside.

Feeling her sex around the head of my shaft, still clenching in orgasm, nearly causes me to lose it. But gritting my teeth in the hope that it will keep me grounded, I push further inside her until I'm met with her resistance.

I stop and meet her gaze. My heart is doing crazy things inside my chest as my balls are screaming out for me to finish. Going down to my elbows, I lick and kiss her nipples and feel them quiver at my touch. She's so damn gorgeous.

Lifting my head, I meet her lips and tongue in a passion and lust fuelled kiss as her legs wrap around my waist and she arches into me.

She goes tense in my arms.

I'm through. *Fuck! Fuck!*

"Give me a minute," she requests, sounding breathless.

My dick is all the way inside her and she wants a minute! Probably to catch her breath from the pain that I'm sure she felt. I just wish I wasn't so worked up because staying put is killing me. I'm twitching inside her and desperately need to move but the less pain I cause her the better.

To try and ease the pain for her, I start playing with her nipples. Rubbing them between my finger and thumb. Taking her lips in another kiss, I continue to massage her nipples and feel her start to loosen up before I feel the slide of my cock as she moves under me.

Raising myself up again, I slowly pull most of the way out and then just as slowly slide all the way back inside her warm sheath—*home.*

"You're finally inside me," she says in wonder.

"I am."

"You feel so good." She flexes her inner muscles around me. "Oh God. That felt good." So she does it again.

"I'm holding on by a thread and you decide to experiment," I growl in passion.

I see the realization in her eyes, the minute it dawns on her what clamping her muscles around me does to me. And she does it a-fuckin'-gain.

"You feel so good inside me."

"No pain?"

She shakes her head. "No, not now. I never want it to end."

"Fuck. I need to move."

Mara rotates her hips sending shards of pleasure down my cock, into the volcano of my balls and it wedges in the base of my spine. My dick swells even more surprising the shit out of me, and Mara, by the startled look on her face.

"I'm close."

"Me too."

That's the only sign I need. Pushing her legs from my waist, I knock her shoes off before she stabs me with one of the lethal heels and hold her legs open wide. I begin to thrust inside her with a rotate of my hips that drives my cock in to the hilt.

Mara throws her head back, gasping for air as I pick up the pace.

My cock is so fuckin' swollen with arousal that it's almost painful. No matter whether I'm thrusting inside or withdrawing, the pleasure is intense. Feeling her sex rippling along my dick is bringing me closer and closer to releasing. The fire in my balls won't be contained for much longer.

I'm sweating and breathing like a freight train and Mara—*fuck me*—is pulling and twisting her nipples between her finger and thumb.

"Babe—"

My eyes roll back in my head as I feel her climax start to rush through her causing mine to explode as though I've been set alight with a match. Gripping her hips, I try to hold her still as my cum flies out and coats her vibrating core. That's how it feels along my cock, as though tiny fingers are massaging along its length causing a vibration.

Opening my eyes, I gaze down at the girl milking my cock dry and my heart bursts. I collapse on top of her and taking her mouth in a sweet kiss, I shiver.

"That was so worth the wait," I mumble against her neck.

"I wish we'd done it sooner. That was like nothing I've ever felt before."

Sliding my now spent dick from her, I roll onto my side and take her with me. I love having my arms wrapped around her and I always will if I have a say in anything.

I kiss her on the forehead and tell her, "I'm going to run you a bath soon, and hopefully the soreness won't be as bad."

"A bath would be nice, but I'll probably be okay because I've brought a bottle of Aloe Vera. It better work the wonders it promises considering what I have planned for you at the carnival tonight."

"What?"

"It's a surprise."

"Mara, babe. As much as I want to be inside you again today, it's not such a good idea."

"We'll see."

I smile. "Are you really happy, Mara? Do you really want to be with me?"

"Where is this coming from?" She brushes the hair from my forehead in a gentle caress. "I love you, Donovan." She kisses me. "I'm the happiest

I've ever been when I'm with you. Please don't ever doubt that. I can't wait to start our life together living in your home—"

"Our home," I interrupt.

"Our home. This is real for me Donovan. I'm old enough to know my own feelings so don't ever think I'm doing something that I'm not ready for because I'm more than ready. I know what I want and that is you."

I have to swallow a few times to get my emotions under control, and also to plan what I want to say to her because all words have flown out of my head.

Instead, I roll over her and opening my drawer, I take out my mothers ring. She gasps when she sees it.

Lying back down, I cover her mouth so she'll let me speak.

"I'm not asking you to marry, yet. You heard me say *yet*, right?" She nods so I continue, "This was my mom's ring and I want you to wear it as a promise ring for now. Because regardless of what I've gotten up to in the past I want something on your finger to show every other fucker that you belong to me. I want everyone to know how serious I am about you. I want you to know that I'm promising to love, honor and cherish you," I smile, "until we say those words in front of a justice of the peace once you've finished your studies." She giggles beneath my hand. "Stop that. And I mean the first course you're doing. I'm sure we can manage a wedding between one course and your doctorate."

"How—"

"You're too clever baby to not study to a higher level."

"I can't believe all this," she says.

I slide the ring on her wedding finger and think *take that you fuckers, she's mine for all time.*

"I love you. You know me like no one else."

"I love you too baby, which means you have to protect me from Reece when he sees you wearing my mom's ring."

"He'll be fine, and I'm going to be okay later and ready to have you inside me again."

"You're an impatient little thing."

"No I'm not. I've just discovered how it feels to finally have sex with the man I love."

"Mara," I growl.

Smiling, she grabs my head and places a sloppy kiss on my face. "You're going to fuck me at the carnival," she informs me before rolling from the bed and walking to the bathroom.

Rolling onto my back, I try to figure out if she's serious or not. Surely she can't mean that. The carnival is only a couple of blocks away and we have a perfectly good bed here. And there is no way she's showing her attributes to every Tom, Dick and Harry. She's trying to get me going again. Isn't she?

Looking down my body, my cock jerks against my stomach already starting to swell again with arousal for the sassiest girl I've ever known.

34

MARA

"Hey Donovan," I shout over to where he's standing talking to Ryder while I savor the warm, pink, fluffy cotton candy he bought me.

"Yeah, babe."

"Will you come and make out with me on the Ferris wheel?"

He does a double take at my words and grins while Ryder shakes his head at him laughing.

Ryder and Dal arrived a couple of hours ago after Reece called them to get their butts to Orange Beach. I'm glad as well. Since they've been here, Dal looks to be happier than I've seen her. I'm not too sure whether that has anything to do with Ryder or the fact she's away from everything back home. I'm hoping it's because she's here having fun with us, and Ryder. Even though I can't quite work out their relationship. Every now and again, he'll touch her back or arm, but nothing more. Perhaps a push together might get them seeing more action.

I grin liking this idea. I've never played matchmaker before so this could be fun.

"What are you grinning at? Looking so lost in thought," Donovan asks moving in close with his hands going to my hips.

"Just thinking," I reply against his lips.

Moving my head to one side, I give him access to my neck. He trails his lips down to my collarbone, and mumbles against my skin, "Let's go make out," he nibbles my ear lobe sending a bout of lust straight to my core, "on the Ferris wheel."

"Mmmm, I thought we were already making out."

He chuckles against my sensitive skin. "You haven't seen anything yet."

Releasing me, he grabs my hand and, with a slight tug, pulls me toward the bright lights of the Ferris wheel.

The carnival is packed with people tonight, which isn't surprising considering the location, but none the less people have come out in droves.

I'm glad the guys suggested this because it's been a few years since I was last at a carnival and

I've forgotten how much fun they are. And how yummy their corn dogs and cotton candy are.

As we approach the Ferris wheel, I come to a stop and stand watching it go round. It's exciting—the music, the lights, the whole design of the wheel, which looks to be in the fifties style. It's beautiful.

Donovan slips his arms around my waist from behind and rests his head on my shoulder. "Are you okay?"

"I'm better than okay. I'm excited we're here. I'd forgotten how much I loved the carnival with all the noise, lights and food."

"Trust you to mention the food," he chuckles.

"Hey. There's nothing like eating carnival food."

I turn in his arms.

"I bet if you tasted me right now, you'd be able to taste the cotton candy I've just finished."

He groans. "You're going to kill me."

I rub up against him and feel the bulge behind his zipper.

"Taste me Dono—"

I don't finish. His mouth is on mine. His hands grip my hips to hold me against him or keep me still —I'm not sure which. I'm not the only one who tastes of cotton candy. He tastes delicious and I want more. Reaching up, my hands grip the back of his neck as I try to climb up him. His tongue imitating what he does with his dick inside my sex, which is clenching with need.

"That's getting pretty heated," Jack states causing Donovan and me to break for much needed air.

Looking at Jack, he's grinning. "You do know you're in public? As in, you have a large audience."

As I look around, some people turn away, but yeah, there are a few people around watching us, which is embarrassing.

I bury my face in Donovan's chest and hear him chuckling.

"Thanks, man. That could have been awkward if we'd gotten any further carried away."

"Don't get too carried away on the Ferris wheel. Don't want you falling out," Jack adds, waving over his shoulder as he walks off.

"C'mon babe. It's our turn." Donovan keeps his arm around me as we climb aboard one of the cars on the wheel.

Sitting down, Donovan covers our laps with a blanket. I give him a quizzical look because the night is still humid and doesn't really call for a blanket.

"Be patient, Mara."

The wheel moves slightly to allow the next

couple to climb into one of the cars taking us slightly higher. Donovan wraps his arm around me and pulls me close.

I'm so excited and rest my head in the crook of Donovan's shoulder as he holds me tight.

It isn't long before we actually get moving on our five-minute ride. I love the breeze that's caressing my skin with the movement of the wheel. It doesn't go too fast and with it being dark, we can see all the lights in the distance, even a few boats out at sea.

I love being up here with my man. He feels so good against me. He seems happy to just hold me, but although I'm happy, I'm going to take advantage of the blanket, and touch him.

Caressing down his chest and stomach, I slip my hand under his tee shirt and feel his abs quiver at my touch as my fingers stroke up to his nipples. Rubbing them into tight buds has him shifting slightly. I hope he's rising to the occasion. There is only one way to find out.

Turning my face into his neck, I start to nibble along his jaw. His hand around me tightens as mine slowly makes it's way back down his stomach to rub along the edge of his waistband. Slightly dipping inside, I continue to rub—teasing him.

"Give me your mouth."

I lift to him and lose all thought when his tongue tangles with mine.

My hand slips further inside his jeans, touching the head of his growing shaft. He growls in my mouth as I quickly pull my hand out and undo his zipper before slipping my hand inside again to pull him out. He's hard and fully aroused now in my hand. My core aches to be filled by him, but there isn't anyway that can happen on the Ferris wheel.

Our tongues tangle and mate while I'm stroking his length back and forth. He feels like satin in my hand, all smooth skin and heavily aroused man.

35

DONOVAN

Having Mara's hand wrapped around me is pretty soon going to have me embarrassing myself. Her small hand moving over me is arousing as hell. My balls are pressed tight to my body knowing I'm getting ready to release.

As the wheel takes us up again, I rub her nipples, which are already hard with arousal before moving my hand lower beneath the blanket. I nudge her legs and slide my hand up between her thighs needing to touch her aroused flesh. To my surprise, I find her naked beneath her short skirt.

I growl at the easy access I have to her pussy, and then hiss when she drags a nail through the slit on my dick before she continues jerking me off.

My hand slips between her lips as I coat my fingers in her arousal before I start to circle her entrance with a finger. Pushing inside her, she catches her breath and moans, her core clamps around my fingers as her hips start moving. *Fuck!* We can't do this on here.

Withdrawing my finger, I pull away from her and break the kiss. "We can't on here." Shit, I can't even catch my breath.

Her hand tightens around my dick as she picks up speed. "You can," she whispers.

"No. Oh God, babe. Stop." I knock her hand away, trying to catch my breath as my dick throbs for relief. But not on the Ferris wheel.

Quickly shoving my cock away before she can grab hold of me again, I sit up straighter and pull her into my arms.

The wheel stops one below us.

That was fuckin' close.

I still can't catch my breath and my balls and dick are aching—giving a new meaning to blue balls.

"That was fun," she smirks.

"We need to find somewhere private as soon as we get off here," I growl. "Because I'm going to get us off just as soon as I can move."

She laughs.

Mara's scrambled my brain.

I can honestly say with all the shit I've done in the past, that I've never had such a hot make out session on a Ferries wheel before. Not even close.

When it's our turn to climb out, I can't meet the guy's knowing eyes so I ignore him and mumbling a thank you, I help Mara out and pull her along with me. I'm not really sure where I'm going until Ryder and Dahlia step out in front of us. Dahlia looking upset.

"Is everything all right?" I ask.

"Yeah," Ryder says.

"No," Dahlia contradicts.

"Um, Dal, do you want to go and get some drinks?" Mara asks giving my hand a squeeze.

"That would be good."

Mara reaches up and kisses me. "I won't be long." She gives me an apologetic look.

"I'll get you back later." I pat her on her sexy butt. "Go look after your sister."

She gives me a saucy grin in return.

Watching them go off chatting, I turn to Ryder. "So what did you do to piss her off?"

He looks pissed, which soon changes as he laughs. "Fuck. What makes you think it was my fault?"

"Because a girl doesn't have that look on her face otherwise."

He shakes his head. "It doesn't matter."

"Really?"

"Yeah, really."

"You do realize that Dahlia will probably tell Mara, who will tell me."

"Fuckin' hell!! It's like a church fuckin' meeting."

"Just spit it out."

"I kissed her."

He kissed her?

"So why is she pissed at you? I thought you'd both been doing plenty of that already."

He starts walking toward where the girls have gone before pulling me up short.

"We haven't done anything. We're trying to be friends, but she's driving me crazy so I kissed her, briefly, then apologized. She couldn't get away from me quick enough."

"You apologized?"

"I know, but my life isn't that straightforward. I took what I've wanted since the first time I saw her, but anything else isn't possible. She needs permanence in her life, and that isn't me. Anymore. So I stopped."

He looks pained.

"What can be so bad that you can't even contemplate a relationship with her?" I laugh. I never thought I'd be giving relationship advice. "You want more with her that's why you stopped and didn't just go for the one night. Is that right?"

He nods dragging his hand down his face.

"For the first time in six years I've met someone who makes my heart lighter. She makes me forget, but when I remember, it's like being shot through the chest." He rubs his chest as we both watch the girls approaching laden down with drinks.

I grin when I spot the corn dog in my girl's hand. She's going to be sick if she eats anything else.

Ryder clears his throat. "I know I was kind of cryptic, but can we keep what I've said between us?"

"No problem."

36

MARA

DONOVAN IS DRIVING ME CRAZY. AS WE WALKED into the hotel, there appeared to be a wedding taking place toward the back. He grinned at me, took my hand and dragged me into the marquee where there is a live band and a crowded dance floor.

His hands are everywhere and nowhere. We've been on the dance floor now for three songs. He knows what he's doing to me as well because he keeps smirking. At this rate I'm going to end up knocking the smirk off his face. His hands have been all over me, but he's avoiding where I want his touch the most.

He's going to touch me where I need him to if it's the last thing he does. He thinks he's being noble after he's *deflowered* me, well he isn't—he's frustrating the hell out of me.

The lights dip so now it's time to knock him on his ass. Straddling his thigh, I get as close as I possibly can and feel the bulge going on in his jeans. I start to rock against him. His hand lands on my bottom, squeezing and pushing me into him. Moaning in his ear, I feel his cock swell even more.

My core throbs to have him inside me again and my knees nearly buckle when I feel his hands beneath my skirt, inching closer and closer to my naked ass.

He has a death grip on my butt so feeling adventurous, I shove my hand straight down the front of his jeans and stroke his naked flesh.

Then we're moving—out through the marquee.

He slaps a quick kiss to my lips before pulling me along behind him as he leads us to our room.

As soon as our door shuts, he's on me. Our mouths seal together, his hands shove my skirt up to my waist. One hand slides onto my butt and the other rubs my pussy.

We break from the kiss, gasping for air.

"I can't believe you didn't put any panties on."

"Don't talk. Fuck me."

He pauses before quickly dropping his zipper to free his erection.

Before I can blink, I'm back in his arms and being hoisted up, my legs go around his waist and he's pushing inside me—dropping me down on top of him.

There is a slight discomfort, but nothing to stop me right now. I want and need him inside me.

He pins me to the wall with his cock so deep inside me that I'm sure he's prodding the entrance to my womb. He hisses, "You drive me crazy," as he drops his head and takes my mouth in a heated kiss.

His hips start moving as our tongues tangle and caress. My climax is fast approaching as he stops and lifts me off him.

"No."

"Hang on baby. We're stripping and hitting the shower. I want you all slippery in my arms."

"My arm."

"Shit. I forgot about that. Um. I know."

Before I know it our clothes are thrown all over the room, I have a plastic bag wrapped tightly around the plaster cast leaving my fingers free, and he has us inside the shower with the water pelting down on us.

The way he looks at me, as though he wants me for dinner, causes my heart to beat frantically in my chest.

Taking hold of the shower gel, he squirts a large

amount into his hands before moving closer and caressing down from my collarbone and over my breasts with his magic hands. As he concentrates around my nipples, I throw my head back and moan. The sensation shoots straight between my thighs. Then his hands are on the move again as he rubs the gel into my stomach, moving further south as he strokes my pussy. My legs quiver from his arousing touch.

"You are so damn hot, Mara. I have no idea where to sample you first."

I grin and drop to my knees. He's so sexy clothed, but unclothed he's scorching, and with water cascading down his muscular body, well, I really have no words.

Reaching out, I grip the base of his shaft and bring him to my waiting mouth, swirling my tongue around the bulbous head before sucking him into my mouth.

His hands tangle in my hair while my head bobs up and down on him. I stroke up his thigh with my other hand and feel his legs start to shake as I gently squeeze his balls.

"Enough," he growls pulling me off him.

He pulls me up and, finding my feet, he turns me around and places my hands on the shower wall in front of me and pulls my bottom out toward him.

"You're so fuckin' sexy." He lightly smacks me on the ass. The smack sounds louder because of the water, and he does it again before I feel his mouth on me.

He spreads my cheeks wide and enters me in one go.

"Oh, shit. Mara. That feels good, baby."

Cupping my breasts, he twists and tugs at my nipples while thrusting in and out of me. Because of the angle his balls slap against my pussy heightening my arousal. Every cell in my body is sizzling. The excitement of being with Donovan, and having him buried so deep, lost in lust and love for me is driving me higher and higher, until he stops moving and grinds against me. I explode. I see stars. I never want him to stop. I'm clenching Donovan so strongly with my orgasm that I feel his own release shoot out of him. Strong jerks of his cock as he coats the inside of my sex.

Groaning, I throw my head back, not wanting this to end. I look up and let the water from the shower caress over my face as the pleasure slowly starts to subside, but leaves small tremors running through me as Donovan slowly slides back and forth before he withdraws completely.

I can't move as he quickly cleans me up before

switching the shower off. He pulls me into his arms and wraps me up in a large, fluffy towel.

"One minute." He sits me on the vanity unit while he quickly dries and wraps a towel around his hips. "Let me take the plastic off and then I'm going to put you to bed."

I smile. He's always taking care of me.

EPILOGUE

6 WEEKS LATER

Donovan

Since our trip to the beach with the guys and their girls Mara and I have been living wrapped in our own bubble for want of better words. Apart from a few times when the guys and their wives have come calling now that they are back in Alabama as well.

No sooner had we returned from the beach than we'd moved all our belongings from the city to our home in the heart of Alabama. And nothing has ever felt so right. I feel as though my life is complete now. I have the woman who has my heart in my life permanently.

She's amazing and is so strong and has no qualms about fighting for what she wants or believes in. Right now that appears to be me, and you will never hear any complaints from me.

Even Reece has stopped glaring at me when he sees us together, even when we're wrapped up in each other. The place I like to be the most.

As for Mara's friend, Harry, he wasn't impressed when Mara told him she was 'promised' to me, and moving back home. The dick had tried to talk her out of it, which I'd overheard. Mara had finally told him that she only ever considered him a friend, and nothing more because she'd lost her heart to me two years before.

Hearing her admit it out loud to someone else made me feel good, although I did have a few seconds of feeling sorry for the poor bastard.

It was with relief when we finally arrived back here with all our belongings and spent the first night in our home knowing that we were together.

And now I'm stretched out in the hammock out back watching a couple of boats on the lake with a longneck in my hand wishing my girl was here with me. Instead she is in town with Dahlia shopping for my birthday, which is tomorrow. Our age difference doesn't bother me as much as it did because I love her too damn much to even contemplate it anymore.

Sighing, I take a long drink from the bottle while I think about the architectural course I've just found out I've been accepted to. I have to wait a few months before it starts because of the timing, but it feels good knowing that I'm about to take my life in a different direction than what was planned for me. Part of my decision makes me feel sad, as though I'm going to be disappointing my dad, but like Mara says, he loved me and at the end of the day he would want me to be happy. He wouldn't like knowing how tormented I am over a decision that in the long run is what I desperately want. So I'm going back to college with my girl. I've already warned her that I plan on doing a lot of making out while we're there so that we'll fit in perfectly on campus. I don't think she believes me though. We'll see!

Hearing a car come to a stop outside puts a stop to my musing. I stay put hoping it's my girl so that she'll join me in the hammock. Some of the best sex between us has taken place on this hammock. Nothing like having a lazy afternoon of love making with your girl sitting astride you, riding your cock while her breasts sway with the movement.

It's so not a good idea having these thoughts while I'm waiting to discover whether it's my girl or someone else visiting. Mara's eyes will light up seeing me hard and ready for her, but someone else, then it could get embarrassing, especially if it's Mara's mom, Cindy. I cringe with that thought.

Mara

I'M EXCITED TO BE FINALLY HOME FROM THE shopping trip into town with Dahlia. Until today I had no idea that she was so difficult to shop with. The trip was to find her a dress to wear on her first date with Ryder, plus I wanted to purchase a surprise for Donovan for his birthday tomorrow. After two hours of trying things on she finally found the perfect dress in a purple and white silk. It was beautiful and so were the high heels to match. I just hope she doesn't break her neck in the shoes. Providing the date goes ahead.

They've both been dancing around each other these past few weeks, more so than before Reece's wedding so it's about time Ryder finally worked up to asking her out to dinner. I'm not sure what's going on though. Something is and I believe Dahlia when she says she has no idea why he goes hot and cold. I guess only time will tell.

Walking around the side of the house, I come to a stop and smile when I see the love of my life relaxing in the hammock with his drink of choice in his hand and a book open on his stomach.

"You're a sight for sore eyes, baby. Come and join me," he invites, smiling.

How can I refuse my sexy guy?

Getting settled with him in the hammock, I wrap my arm around his stomach and snuggle into him. He's so comfortable that I'm not sure I'll be able to move later. I love coming home to him and never want that to change. He makes me giddy with the love I have for him and the love he throws at me all the time.

Bending my knee, I bring it up on to his lap, which is my usual position. And as usual he's hard for me. I hope that never changes as I wiggle a bit closer.

He groans. "Stop that. I want to enjoy holding you for a while. I missed you this afternoon." He kisses me on my forehead.

"I missed you as well, but it was worth the trip. I

got you a fantastic present, which you can't have until tomorrow."

He hates surprises.

"You'll tell me before then."

"No I won't."

"Yes you will. Because I can play dirty and refuse to let you come until you've told me," he smirks.

"You always play dirty and I love it." I rise up slightly and kiss him on the lips. "I never knew what dirty sex was until I met you. You have a lot to answer for."

"You complaining?"

"Never," I chuckle. "I'm planning on getting down and dirty with you in the morning to celebrate your birthday in style."

"Mmm. Sounds good babe. Are we still going to meet the guys and their wives tonight?"

I pinch him. "That was a quick change of subject."

"I need to think about something else, otherwise we won't be going anywhere."

"I should have known, and yes, we're meeting them later at Kix."

Which reminds me. "When I dropped Dal off at Kix there was an older woman we haven't seen before. As Ryder walked down the steps out front to come over to us, she climbed out of her car and threw herself into Ryder's arms. From the shocked look on his face she was unexpected. I couldn't decide whether the hug looked innocent, like perhaps she was his Mom, or whether she was someone Dal needed to worry about. Dal looked nervous, but insisted I head back to you. I feel as though I should have stayed with her. That she might be in need of some support." I shrug. "But I really didn't know what to make of it. Has he said anything to you?"

I move to straddle him—my favorite position.

His eyes narrow.

"He has only ever mentioned that his past is screwed up, which is preventing him from being with Dahlia. He seemed torn up about it because he really wants to be with her. And what are you doing?" he asks as I start rocking against him.

"I need you."

"Hmm." Donovan pulls me down so he can reach my mouth and kisses me. "If we're going out, we need to shower and change."

"Shower?"

"Trust you to pick out that one word."

I smirk, wrapping myself around him as much as I can in the hammock and bury my face in his neck. "Thank you for making me so happy. For loving me. I love you so much Donovan." I finish nibbling on his earlobe.

"Stop that."

As I start to rise back into a sitting position, he cups my face in his hands and tells me, "You're everything to me, Mara. Don't ever forget that."

"I won't," I reply, tears in my voice.

THE END

Thank you for reading *My Best Friend's Sister: Sultry,* and thank you for your reviews! It's really appreciated.

Subscribe with your email to be alerted about new releases, sales, and events.
http://ronajameson.com/suscribe

NEVER LET GO: SAVOR, BAD BOY ROCKERS #4

PROLOGUE

Ryder

At the carnival...

Watching Dahlia—or Dal, as Reece and Mara call her—walk toward me, my heart practically leaps out of my chest. She's breathtaking; her long, sexy legs going on for miles in her little shorts and cowgirl boots. Her snug tee shirt in the purple silk caresses her large breasts and makes my mouth water. Coming to a stop in front of me, she passes me a Pepsi and as our fingers touch, a bolt of desire hits me square in the balls.

"Thanks," I reply, hoping to make eye contact with her.

She meets my gaze and seems to be waiting for some kind of signal from me, which I give with a smile. Letting her know we're good, even though it was me being a dick before that caused her to get bent out of shape.

I really need to talk to her, but I'm not sure what the hell to say—to explain why we can't be involved. For the first time in my life, I've met someone I want a lot more from, but I'm too damn honorable to do anything about it.

I've met other women in the past who have tempted me, hey, I'm a red-blooded guy after all, but I always pushed that temptation away—no matter how much those women begged for my attention. Any urges I have, I take care of with my hand and I have done so for a hell of a long time.

Dahlia is different though. I want her with a passion I've never known, and her presence torments me like nothing ever has before. I sure as hell don't want to think about how I'll react if there's ever another guy sniffing around her. That won't go down too well.

Donovan nudges me, breaking into my thoughts. "We're heading back to the hotel. We'll see you guys tomorrow."

I vaguely hear him as my attention is still on Dahlia. The way her mahogany hair falls down her back and over her shoulders to the tips of her breasts. She has freckles over her nose and cheek-bones making her look like the girl next door. She takes my breath away every time I look at her. When we first met, my opinion of her wasn't all that good, but that soon changed when Reece put me straight.

All we are ever going to have is friendship, and that's only if I don't screw it up. Grimacing, I realize that's not going to happen—I screw everything up.

Six years ago, I was still in the Marines and should have known better. I made a huge mistake and now I have to live with it, when all I want to do is build something with the woman standing in front of me.

"You really are beautiful," I blurt out.

Her eyes widen in surprise before sadness crosses her features. "Don't Ryder. Just don't, okay? It was a mistake before, so let's just forget it. I don't have many friends and I don't want to lose you."

Fuck!

"I don't have anything to say other than I'll try." My eyes search hers, searching for something more than friendship but I can't see it. Finally, I finish, "I'm sorry, but my life is a mess."

She slides her hand into mine.

"So is mine. C'mon. Teach me to shoot."

Dahlia

My hand trembles as I take hold of Ryder's and I cling to his in an effort to keep him close to me. I can't help worry that he'll refuse me, but to my relief he doesn't.

The kiss we shared not too long ago was hot and exciting. I didn't want it to end, but he quickly pulled away and apologized for kissing me. It hurts a lot when I've dreamed of him kissing me since we first met.

There's something about Ryder that calls to me. He seems lonely, which first attracted me to him. Not that there's anything wrong with the rest of him. His muscular chest and six-pack abs are drool worthy. Combine that with his tight buns and strong legs and his body makes me wonder why he isn't swarmed with women daily. He might be cute as well, but we won't mention that.

Sometimes he looks at me as though I'm the only one he sees. The way Reece looks at Callie. But Ryder never does anything about it. He's hinted more than once that he has a screwed up past, but he won't say anything else.

I'd be lying if I didn't admit I was curious. Who wouldn't be? I just wish he'd tell me so I knew why he wouldn't take our obvious attraction to the next level. I mean, how bad could his past be? Everyone has something screwed up in their past and I'm no different.

As we approach the shooting range, his thumb begins caressing mine, and I don't think he realizes he's doing it. I'm not about to complain because the pleasure of his touch causes my heart to beat faster. I have no wish to let go of him, but as the guy looking after the stalls approaches us, I'm not going to have a choice if I want to win one of the large bears. My shooting skills aren't that bad, thanks to Reece, but I might have to do some acting, and hopefully, I'll get Ryder's arms around me as he shows me the proper stance to shoot those ducks.

"How many?" the guy asks.

"Just my girl," Ryder replies, and my heart does a leap of joy.

Just my girl! Is this how he thinks of me?

Ryder pays the guy before turning his attention back to me. "Do you know what you're doing here?"

A little white lie is okay, right? "Not really. Will you show me?"

I hold his gaze while he decides whether I'm being serious or not before he finally gives in with a sigh.

"C'mon. Take hold of this." He passes me the air rifle. "Now relax." He steps in behind me and runs his arms from my shoulders to my hands. He keeps one hand around mine on the weapon and his other hand resting on my hip.

Everyone else disappears as my senses take over and his heat envelopes me. I lean into it, a soft sigh on my lips as I fight the urge to roll against him. "Dahlia," he whispers against my ear. Goose bumps break out on my skin as his breath caresses me like silk.

I turn my head to face him, and not realizing just how close he is to me, my lips brush against his. My eyes immediately shoot up to his, as Ryder's hand contracts on my hip.

Available online: Never Let Go: Savor

ACKNOWLEDGMENTS

Cover Design: Robin Harper, Wicked by Design

Editor: Sirena Van Schaik

OTHER BOOKS BY LEXI BUCHANAN

Bad Boy Rockers

Book 1: My Brother's Girl (Sizzle) (Jack 'Jack' & Thalia)

Book 2: Past Sins (Spicy) (Reece & Callie)

Book 3: My Best Friend's Sister (Sultry) (Donovan & Mara)

Book 4: Never Let Go (Savor) (Ryder & Dahlia)

Book 5: Saving Jace (Sinful) (Jace & Savannah)

Book 6: Silent Night (Novella)

Kincaid Sisters

Book 1: Meant to be Mine

Book 2: You Were Always Mine (coming soon)

Book 3: Will You be Mine (coming soon)

McKenzie Brothers

Book 1: Seduce (Michael & Lily)

Book 1.5: The Wedding (Novella)

Book 2: Rapture (Sebastian & Carla)

Book 3: Delight (Ruben & Rosie)

Book 4: *Entice (Lucien & Sabrina)*

Book 5: *Cherished (Ramon & Noah)*

Book 5.5: *A McKenzie Christmas (Novella)*

De La Fuente Family (McKenzie Spinoff)

Book 1: *Love in Montana (Sylvia & Eric)*

Book 2: *Love in Purgatory (Dante & Emelia)*

Book 3: *Love in Bloom (Mateo & Erin)*

Book 4: *Love in Country (Aiden & Sarah)*

Book 5: *Love in Flame (Diego & Rae)*

Book 6: *Love in Game (Kasey & Felicity)*

Book 7: *Love in Education (Andie & Seth)*

McKenzie Cousins

(McKenzie Spinoff)

Book 1: *Baby Makes Three (Sirena & Garrett)*

Book 2: *A Business Decision (Michael & Brooke)*

Book 3: *Secret Kisses (Charlotte & Tanner)*

Book 4: *Kissing Cousins (Rachel & Alexander)*

Book 5: *If Only (Madison & Derek)*

Book 6: *Princess & the Puck (Paige & Seth)*

Book 7: *A Bakers Delight (Sofia & Shane)*

Book 8: *A Cowboy for Christmas (Olivia & Geary)*

Book 9: *A Secret Affair (Joshua & Mallory)*

Book 10: *One Christmas (Dylan & Jenna)*

Book 11: *The Pregnant Professor (Jaxon & Poppy)*

Book 12: *It Started with a Kiss (Ryan & Gretchen)*

Jackson Hole

Book 1: *From This Moment*

Book 1.5: *When we Meet (Novella, in the back of From This Moment)*

Book 2: *New Beginning (coming soon)*

Romantic Suspense

Lawful

Stryker

Standalone Novella's

One Dance

Educate Me

Pure

Holiday Season

Kissing Under the Mistletoe

A Soldier's Christmas

Jingle Bells

Written as Rona Jameson

STRYKER, MMA ROMANTIC SUSPENSE

WRITTEN AS LEXI BUCHANAN

When my childhood friend, Cora, dared me to write a sexy novel about a martial arts fighter, I agreed, albeit under the influence of alcohol. It was something for me—something different and exciting.

It was supposed to be research, pure and simple. But then I met him—a six-foot-six mountain of a man with no name. The way his muscles flexed and rippled when he trained made my belly quiver. The way his dark hair flopped over his forehead made me want to brush it back from his strong face. His nose had been broken, but it made no difference, he was still a handsome man. He had eyes dark as the night that would land on me the minute I entered *his* gym...Every...Time.

He was their star fighter, the one that brought in the big money. At first I feared him because of his size and the way he would look at me. But then I discovered that I was his biggest distraction, and no matter what my head told me, my heart told me to fight for the man who didn't know how to live outside of the octagon.

Available at online retailers.

COME BACK TO ME

WRITTEN AS RONA JAMESON

A whispered plea transcends time.

When Esmé Rogers meets Luke Carlisle in 1987, she never expected to end up on board the Titanic for its maiden voyage from Southampton to New York in 1912. But what started with confusion and questions turns into the greatest love of her life.

As the date of the ill-fated sinking of the ocean liner approaches, Esmé questions whether or not she should try and change history. However, one question keeps coming back to haunt her: Does she survive?

With frigid waters and a predestined collision on the horizon, can she change the fate of those she loves?

Available at online retailers.

TWENTY EIGHT DAYS, A NERO SOREN NOVEL

WRITTEN AS RONA JAMESON

Sentenced to death...

All hope gone...

Until he receives a visit from victim #6

Condemned for a crime he didn't commit, Quinten Peterson sat on death row praying for a miracle. He just never expected his angel of mercy to be the girl he fell in love with so long ago.

The press called her a victim, but Saige Lockwood was a survivor. And she had twenty-eight days to discover the truth about what really happened to her that fateful night, eight years ago.

With time running out, Saige desperately needed to unlock her memories . . . before it was too late.

Available at online retailers.

THE NEXT VICTIM, A NERO SOREN NOVEL

WRITTEN AS RONA JAMESON

For nine years Faye Ingram had lived with the harrowing guilt of what became of her sister. After all it had been her fault that Kelsey had been driving home from college that dark night...*hadn't it?*

Their parents blamed her.

Kelsey's boyfriend blamed her.

Kelsey's friends blamed her.

The killer hadn't only taken her sister from her family and friends; he'd taken Faye's life...and now it was time to claim it back.

FBI Supervisory Special Agent Nero Soren understood Faye's need for answers, except the more questions she asked, the more he feared for her safety. His instincts told him that the killer they hunted was hunting a prey of his own, but was the prey, *Faye Ingram* or *Christina Peterson?*

SSA Nero Soren along with his partner, SSA Logan Reddick, raced to find the killer before he claimed *the next victim.*

2020

Cover Design by Abigail Higson

ABOUT THE AUTHOR

English born Rona Jameson is an author of romance who currently resides in Ireland with her husband, four children, one dog, three cats, and a guinea pig named Merry. She's been writing since 2013 as Lexi Buchanan, which is where you can find her more explicit writing.

Follow on social media:

Website: http://ronajameson.com
Email: authorlexibuchanan@gmail.com

facebook.com/lexibuchananauthor

twitter.com/AuthorLexi

instagram.com/authorlexib

bookbub.com/author/lexi-buchanan

Printed in Great Britain
by Amazon

19819752R00202